BLOOD MOON

ALPHA WOLF ACADEMY: BOOK 3

JJ KING

Kindle Edition
ISBN- 978-1-989794-04-3

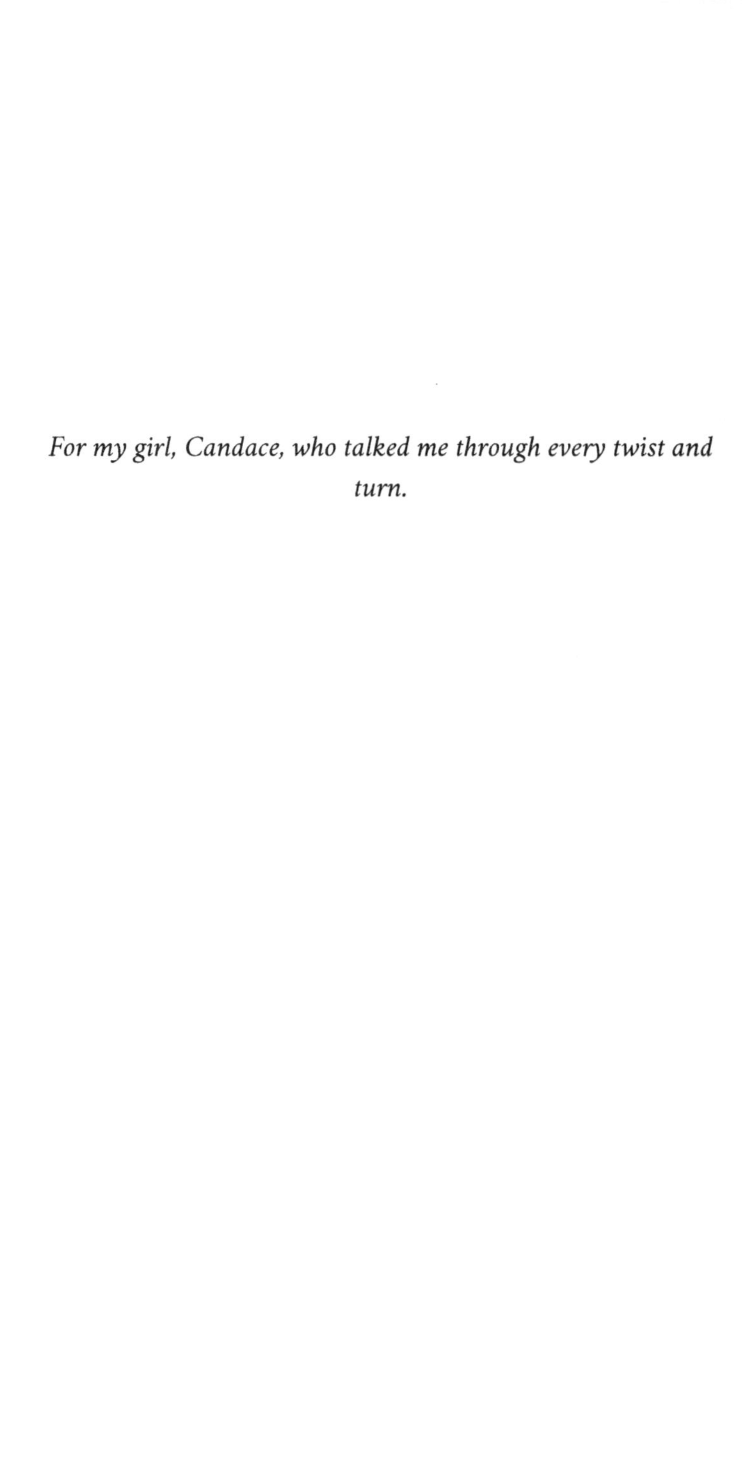

For my girl, Candace, who talked me through every twist and turn.

ACKNOWLEDGMENTS

This one goes out to all the fan girls (and boys). See, I'm a geek. I grew up with two older brothers and followed in their comic book & epic fantasy loving footsteps. I love Star Wars, Star Trek, Star Gate, and Battlestar Galactica. Give me a "star" and I'm there! I also adore Buffy the Vampire Slayer, The Vampire Diaries, and Twilight.

What I'm saying is, I'm a geek.

So, this one is for my fellow geeks and freaks, who just love disappearing into another world. I hope I've created a world you can slip into and adore.

CHAPTER 1

Sweat dripped into my eyes, stinging them, blurring them, but I ignored it and kept my focus locked on the man standing across from me. His eyes were narrowed and his stance ready to strike out. I watched his gaze, measuring his intentions rather than reacting to his movements, as I'd been taught, as I'd been practicing.

A wicked grin lifted my lips, baring my teeth as I paced to my left, legs crossing smoothly so my body stayed centered, balanced, ready.

When he decided to strike, his eyes shifted, ever so slightly. I ducked, moving my body into a dance that moved me out of arm's reach, out of danger. Still in fluid motion, I pulled my fists in tight, rotated my core, and snapped a leg out with a roar of exertion.

His eyes went wide for a split second, then dark as he tumbled to the sparring mat in a heap of muscles and sweat. He sat there, head swaying, saying nothing for a moment while he pulled out his teeth guard and undid the strap to his helmet.

"You almost knocked me out," he said in a voice edged with disbelief. When his dark gaze lifted to mine, though, there was only pride coloring them. "Damn good job, Elena." Tomas climbed to his feet on unsteady legs and clapped a hand to my shoulder for support, which I graciously gave with a huge grin. "Down girl," he muttered with a chuckle.

"Never," I retorted, pretending to deliver a jab to his midsection.

Tomas grimaced and shook his head. "Not ready for another round yet." He lifted a hand to his head and blinked slowly as if trying to dislodge the cobwebs there. "Maybe not for a while."

I left him swaying and went to retrieve our water bottles and towels from the nearby bench. "Here." I tossed him the towel first and waited while he mopped up his face to pass him the bottle. My water tasted like ambrosia as I chugged it greedily.

I moved to the wall of mirrors and picked up two twenty-pound dumbbells. "Where did you learn krav maga like that?" I asked, lifting the weights slowly to my shoulders then back to my waist while I studied my new trainer's reflection.

He was good, I'd known that the first time we'd sparred. Since Anthony LaFlamme had Alpha responsibilities, not to mention a wife and children, he'd sent one of his most trusted men to train me in the ways of the Jedi. When Tomas had shown up the week after the plane crash, I'd been nervous but excited to meet him.

In truth, he'd saved me. After the plane crash, while most of the others had headed home to recover and move through the stages of guilt and grief, I'd stayed at Alpha Wolf Academy because I didn't have much choice in the matter. My uncle Viktor, the Alpha of Russia, had gotten too close for comfort once again in his quest to murder me like he had my entire family.

I'd been slowly slipping back into the chasm of survivor's guilt that had started tearing me down since I'd learned the truth of the attack on campus back almost a year ago when Tomas had knocked on my door.

I blinked at my reflection in the mirror as that realization struck me. Almost a year had passed since Viktor had destroyed the illusion of safety in my life. In all our lives. Everyone on campus had been rocked and most had lost someone. The guilt had been overwhelming, even with counseling, and had only gotten worse, despite my efforts to the contrary, after Viktor had taken down the plane I'd been on with a bomb. I'd survived, again, while others had died.

Tomas had spared no bullshit in confronting me on the topic. I'd been strong enough to survive, he'd said, but it wasn't enough to just survive. I would have to be strong enough now to actually live. That's when I'd started fighting back.

Something had shifted in me when my Alpha voice had manifested, and I needed to learn more about it, about me and what my body and mind could do.

"Have you talked to Bash yet?" Tomas called out as he pulled his shirt over his head and tossed it into his bag. His defined muscles gleamed with sweat. I admired them, not from sexual curiosity, I had Bash for that, but from a new knowledge of what it took to achieve that level of definition. I was finally starting to use my body to its fullest capabilities and was getting stronger every day. I turned my gaze back to the mirror, to the definition in my arms that hadn't been there before, and grinned.

I bit down on the edge of my lip and finished my last rep, then laid down the weights and reached for my towel again. "I've seen him, but we haven't talked," I said with a heavy sigh. "Not really. And the longer we go, the worse it gets."

"Then have it out with him. Maybe what the two of you need is a good fight." Tomas grinned and gestured to the mat behind them. "Get him here. Make it a literal fight. It'll be good for you both."

I considered his advice. Things had been weirdly formal between Bash and I for a while now, as if we were constantly walking on eggshells, trying to avoid the obvious conversation. He'd been pulled away by family obligations over spring break, while I'd been splashing in the ocean with my parents and friends. I'd come back to AWA tanned and toned with most of my personal relationships in a good place while he'd come back with tight shoulders and eyes dark with strain and stress.

Maybe a good fight is exactly what we need.

I reached my hands into the air above my head, stretching out all my muscles, and arched back with a groan. It was early, barely 6:00 am, so I'd have to wait to instigate our little confrontation. I'd gotten used to waking with the sun over the three-week break and found I liked the quiet of the day before the world awoke.

"I'm going to do a few laps around campus. You up for it, old man?" I arched an eyebrow at him speculatively and grinned, then sat on the mat to pull on my sneakers.

He tossed his towel at me and I dodged it with a laugh. "I'll give you old man," he muttered. "But, no, I can't this morning. I have a video chat scheduled with Anthony in an hour."

"Don't you mean Alpha LaFlamme?" I asked in mock seriousness.

Tomas shook his head. "It's still weird to call him that. He deserves it, he's a great Alpha but I can't help it. I'll always think of Pierre as my Alpha."

"What about Sylvie?" I rose to my feet and pulled on the lightweight jacket.

"We're lucky to have her," Tomas said earnestly. "The LaFlammes are good people."

I nodded in agreement. He was right, they were good people. Before the attack, I'd known there were people who were nicer than others, kinder, smarter, whatever. I just hadn't realized that some people had evil inside them, actual evil, not the "I'm annoyed with you so I'm going to be shitty" kind of emotion. Viktor had willingly snuffed out innocent lives for power and was intent on blowing up anyone who stood in his way now.

Too bad that person was me.

"See you tomorrow morning, then," I said, heading towards the door. I wanted to run while my muscles were still warm and limber. I pulled my earbuds from my pocket, turned on my favorite mix, and popped them in.

The air was warm with the promise of heat. The quad

would be filled with students soon but, for now, it was just me, the flowers, and Imagine Dragons.

I fell into a rhythm that matched the beat of my heart. It was meditative, I'd found, sometimes almost hypnotic, and my favorite time for deep thought. I'd worked through a lot of personal hang-ups on the trails of my island getaway.

I missed my friends and family, but it was nice knowing they were happy and safe. Sara and Bethany had been offered spots at Alpha Wolf Academy with me, courtesy of The Sisterhood, but they'd discussed it in length and had decided that they'd prefer island life while they could get it. The tutors employed by The Sisterhood would ensure they kept up their education while they kept up their tans.

I couldn't blame them, even though my heart had leaped at the thought of having them close. From their perspective, AWA had come under siege and had one of its planes blown up with me on it. They'd begged me to take time off and stay with them, it was safer they'd said. They were right, of course, it probably would be safer, but I had responsibilities and had to be at AWA to fulfill them.

Plus, my soul was incomplete without my mate and he was here.

The Sisterhood was becoming a bigger part of my life. I'd attended another meeting with Sylvie and Katherine and had met more important women than I could keep straight. It sometimes felt like a blur, too much in too short a time.

That was the crux of it, though, time. Most Alphas had a lifetime to prepare and learn about the responsibilities and expectations of ruling a pack and I'd only just begun. I had so much to learn, the pressure of it sometimes felt like a vise pressing in on my chest.

It was tempting to give into the dream that this had never happened, that I was a normal wolf, free to live my life. That wasn't my reality anymore, though, and I was getting better at accepting that. Viktor would never stop hunting me, so I could either hide for the rest of my life or fight back and win. Katherine was a big help in that area. She knew what it was like having a mad man focused on you.

Sylvie and Katherine were a blessing in the midst of all this mess. They'd become like family to me. Mom had just about lost her mind when we'd visited Wild River at the end of our island vacation but, once she'd gotten to know the Alpha as a real person, they'd made friends quickly. It was probably killing her bit by bit that she couldn't brag about her new friend to everyone back home but, as far as they knew, my parents had gotten jobs out west and were living normal lives just like everyone else.

I picked up my pace as the music changed from slow to manic, grinning as my body responded to my will, strong and fast. Adrenaline and endorphins kicked into high gear, filling me with a sense of weightlessness as I bounded around the corner of an old brick building…

… and straight into someone dressed all in black.

CHAPTER 2

I bounced off the hard chest and flew back, arms thrown wide in a futile attempt to catch my balance. Before I could hit the ground, a hand darted out, only a blur, and grabbed my wrist.

"Old Ones, Elena!" The black hoodie fell back from Bash's face. "Are you okay? I didn't see you coming." He tugged me upright and into his arms.

I automatically wrapped my arms around him and buried my face in the crook of his neck, breathing in the scent of him. I'd missed the simple comfort of being in his arms and wanted to enjoy it before the strain of our problems colored the moment.

He smelled so fucking good, it stirred up all my woefully deprived juices. I tucked into him closer, pressing my body against the hard length of him. The way his body shifted and the smell of arousal that wafted from him a moment later told me he felt the same way.

It was a start, I thought, then decided to go with

Tomas' suggestion of a spar to clear the air. I opened my mouth to ask him when he'd be free.

"Do you, ummm," Bash began slowly, pulling back so I could see the nerves in his emerald eyes. "Are you free for coffee?"

"What? Now?" I asked. I glanced down at my sweaty clothes.

Bash smiled. "How about in half an hour? I'll meet you in the blackberry grove." At my nod, he ran his hands down my arms, linked his hands with mine for a moment, then pulled away until our fingers slid apart.

I watched him disappear in the direction I'd just come from and frowned down at my fingers, where the tingle from his touch was already fading. I pressed them to my mouth and prayed we'd find our way through this then ran as fast as I could towards my room to shower.

I dressed in my school uniform, not knowing if I'd get the chance to get back to my room to change before my first class. In concession to the promised heat, I left my blazer hanging in the closet and went for a thin cardigan, fitted white blouse, and plaid tie to go with the plaid skirt I'd gotten specially tailored to fit my 5'10" height. I added an academy tie pin to bring the whole look together then stared at my reflection in the full-length mirror mounted to the wall.

If someone didn't know the difference, they'd think I belonged, I thought. But I didn't belong, not really. I just didn't belong anywhere else either.

I fluffed my hair once and applied a slick of gloss, wanting to look pretty for Bash, then shook my head at my reflection, grabbed my backpack, and walked out my door.

I found Bash in the blackberry grove, as promised, holding two large coffees from my favorite kiosk on campus. The scent of vanilla wafted out of mine, making me smile. He knew my favorite drink; he knew my favorite candy. He knew me. I took a sip and the warmth from the coffee mixed with love for my mate. I put the cup down on the stone wall and reached for him.

He tasted like blackberries, coffee, and man, a potent mix. I wove my fingers through his dark hair and pulled him down into a searing kiss.

His hands came to my hips and pulled me in as his head tilted to deepen his access to my mouth. Pent up sexual hunger burst out of us both and, for a moment, I lost all sense of place and time and just devoured him.

The chuckle of an older gentleman as he walked by the little tucked away garden with a smiling woman on his arm, broke us apart and brought a rush of blood to my cheeks. I wasn't a prude by any sense of the word, most wolves weren't, but I'd been on the verge of jumping Bash in the middle of campus as the academy woke up around us.

"Good morning," Bash said in a raspy voice in his best attempt at ignoring the obvious pheromones pumping off us both.

Their echoes of "Good morning" floated back to us as they strolled away.

I erupted into a fit of giggles the moment they were out of sight and buried my face in Bash's neck. The way his chest hitched from laughter made my heart warm.

"Maybe we should sit," he suggested, skimming his hands down my arms to pull me back enough to look down at me. His eyes were alive with laughter and arousal.

I retrieved my coffee then sat on the bench tucked into the corner, turning so I could look at him. He never failed to make my blood sing but even without his heart-stopping looks, he had my heart.

He toyed with my free hand absently and sipped his coffee. The tension that had been there for weeks rocketed up again. I chewed on my lip for a moment then decided to bite the proverbial bullet.

"He's gone, Bash." I said quietly and felt my heart sink when his fingers stilled.

He nodded slowly. "I know."

I swallowed and tried to keep myself from tearing up. The bond between us was still growing but it was enough to let me feel what he felt, the uncertainty, the nerves, the doubt. I closed my eyes and focused on sending what I felt to him.

"I know you're sorry." Bash raised his gaze to mine and sighed. "You don't have to be sorry for the kiss. I'm not an asshole, Elena. I know that wasn't your choice."

A chill ran up my spine, chasing away all the heat that had gathered under my skin. It was apparently time to finally talk about it.

"Why did you wait so long to tell me? That's the part I don't understand." His voice was low and thick with emotion that punched out at me. Bash's emerald eyes were tired and shattered when he looked up at me.

I squeezed his hand, terrified to let go in case he

turned away from me. I could feel the heartbreak through our bond, and it swamped me. After the crash, I'd told him the truth of my past with Connor but then he'd been pulled away by his family and I'd taken the time to visit with mine. The thought that he'd been suffering with this heartbreak all this time while I'd been actively ignoring it filled me with guilt.

It hadn't worked, of course. Even trying to pretend things would be alright when I got back, I'd twisted and turned most nights, feeling the weight of Bash's absence hanging over me. I'd focused all my energy into rebuilding my relationships and training, pushing down the fear and doubt that kept rising up at every turn. I'd assumed Bash would do the same until we could talk, but I saw now that it had been eating away at him the entire time. My heart seized painfully.

I took a deep breath to steady myself and whispered the words I'd refused to say since the moment Connor had shown up at Alpha Wolf Academy, "He makes me feel safe."

Bash made a sound like a wounded animal and tried to pull his hand from mine but I held on and kept talking in the hope I could make him understand the painful tug of emotions inside me.

"I love you so much," I rushed the words, needing him to hear me and believe. "Old Ones, Bash, you're my soul, you're my mate. I love you." I put down the coffee and reached to stroke his cheek. "I will always love you. That will never change."

"You loved him." It was a statement, not a question.

I nodded. "Yes."

Bash frowned and lifted his head to look at me. "How does he make you feel safe when he left you, Elena? I can't wrap my head around it. He broke your heart. You said it yourself. He destroyed you. So, how can you stand to have him near? How does he make you feel safer than I do?"

I lowered my gaze, too ashamed to look into his eyes. There was so much hurt and confusion in them, it tore at me. But Bash deserved the truth or, at least, the truth as I understood it, as I'd worked it out. I looked into his eyes. "It's because he left me that I trust him with my life."

Bash's lips twisted in confusion. "What do you mean?"

I said, turning more so that I was directly facing him. "It's taken me a bit of time to come to this, but I think I understand now. The Sisterhood sent him to guard me, to make sure I was safe. He wasn't supposed to become my friend," I inhaled and continued, "or more. He could have lost his job for it, but it happened anyway."

"You think he loved you enough to break the rules and then enough to walk away, is that it?" Bash asked quietly.

Hearing my thoughts aloud from him made them sound twisted and impossible. I chewed on my lip, worrying it over. Was I completely wrong? Was it possible Connor had been playing me from the first moment, from our first kiss? It just didn't make sense for someone like him to jeopardize his entire career on a romance when he could have just as easily stayed away and kept watch.

"Yes," I said, mustering the courage to admit it. "I think he fell in love and made some bad decisions, then walked away because it was the only way he could stay to keep me safe." I closed my eyes and prayed this didn't make things worse between me and Bash.

He was quiet for a long time, so long my skin began to tingle with anxiety. I forced myself to swallow the need to beg him to talk, to tell me what he was feeling. He had the right to time and patience, to think this over before speaking to me about it. I gave him all that but refused to let go of his hand.

"Do you still love him?"

Everything inside me tightened at the rawness of his voice. His fear and confusion were like blades slicing my skin through the bond that connected us. I ignored the tears that streamed from my eyes and focused solely on that bond, on projecting my love, the enormity of it, to him so he could understand just how much he meant to me.

The only man I love is you.

Bash's head snapped up and his eyes, so broken a moment before, widened in shock. I stared back, startled at his reaction to the words I'd yet to say, then gasped as his voice whispered in my mind.

Can you hear my thoughts?

A laugh bubbled out of me, echoing through the silence around us. I slapped a hand to my mouth and just stared at him as my thoughts whirled wildly.

Slow down, I heard Bash's voice say with amusement in my mind. His eyes filled with tears barely held back as he looked into my eyes. *I can hear you.* He raised a hand to my chest and rested it above my heart. *I can feel you. It's alright. I understand now.*

A sob broke from my throat as a tidal wave of relief and love sucked me under. I threw myself into his arms and just held on, unable to do much more than just gasp for breath in his arms. His embrace enveloped me, gathering me so close it felt as if we were one.

I pressed my lips to his neck and reveled in the taste of his skin and my own tears. They were tears of happiness now, so different than the grief that had spilled from me just moments ago. My lips skimmed his jaw, fluttering over the stubble I loved so much to find his mouth.

His fingers delved into my hair and pulled me closer as his mouth devoured my lips. I gasped into him, giving his tongue entrance as words of love and devotion poured from his mind into mine. It was so intimate, hearing him, feeling him, and tasting him all at the same time. It was as if we existed in a private world of our own, a beautiful world where danger and fear no longer existed.

I pulled back an inch so my lips hovered above his and whispered, "Why Mr. Reeves, are you coming onto me?"

His lips turned up easily and his eyes flashed with aroused amusement. "I believe I am, Ms. Jensen. Do you have a problem with that?"

I pursed my lips as if I were considering, then shook my head. "None at all." I linked my arms around his neck and sighed. "I know it's verboten," I said, dipping into my Buffy vocabulary. "But, would you consider skipping class with me to participate in some extracurricular activities?" I leaned into his ear and whispered, "To be clear, I mean sex." I gasped at my naughty suggestion in mock concern.

His eyes went from emerald to near black in an

instant, then he was pulling me up and dragging me back, behind the bushes, into the shadows. My back hit the brick just as his teeth closed over my bottom lip.

I gasped, for real this time, as the nip mixed pain with pleasure. His teeth moved on, to my jaw, my neck, my shoulder, taking small bites along the way, marking me as his hands ran over my body, lighting my nerves on fire.

I closed my eyes and raked my nails through his hair, over his neck, grasping at him in wild abandon, needing everything he was giving and more. When he dropped to his knees in the dirt at my feet and reached beneath my skirt to pull down my lace panties, I forgot how to breathe.

His clever fingers helped me step out of them before he stuffed them into his pocket and hooked one of my legs over his shoulder.

My eyes rolled back so hard at the first touch of his tongue that I thought for sure I must be blind now. I'd take it, I thought, just to be in this moment. My hands slapped against the rough bricks and I searched for something, anything, to hold onto, to keep me from melting to the ground. My remaining leg buckled for an instant, then Bash's hands were at my hip, pinning me to the building as his mouth did unspeakable things.

It was like being burned alive while riding a wave of pure pleasure. I tore a hand from the building wall and plastered it over my mouth in a futile attempt to stifle the screams that wanted to rip out of me. When he added his fingers, sliding them into me as I poised at the edge of release, I came with a breathless gasp and tears that tracked down my cheeks and onto his head.

Bash rose to his feet, pressing the length of his body against me on the way up and fitted his mouth to mine. The taste of my pleasure on his lips almost undid me again. I wanted more, I needed all of him. I reached for his pants buckle.

"Not here," his whisper was rough and smelled of sex. He captured my mouth again and plundered it, licking and biting at my swollen lips as his hands smoothed down my skirt. When he pulled away, his lips were lifted in a wicked grin and echoed in his endlessly emerald eyes. His hands slipped into mine and then we were off, running like wild children towards his room since it was nearest.

My heart pounded in my chest, spurred on by the sense of Bash's voice and emotions in my soul. I concentrated all my thoughts and feelings on him and whispered suggestions, each one dirtier than the last, until a fine sheen of sweat broke out on his face and his eyes went black with desire.

I was giggling over my evil antics when we ran straight into Xavier.

I smacked into Bash's back and nearly cursed before seeing my professor and mentor. An amused look crossed his face as he looked from Bash to me, then he held up a manila envelope and arched an eyebrow.

"I was just looking for you. I've got fifteen minutes to spare. Meet me in my office in two minutes." He walked off without another word leaving me and my hormonally hopped up soul mate standing just fifty feet from Bash's room with no way to relieve the tension swimming in both our veins.

Fuck, I thought as hard as I could then gave Bash a kiss

that made my own head spin. As I stalked off, regretting the run-in with Xavier, I heard Bash's detailed description of what he'd do to me later in my head and pressed my legs together in anticipation.

CHAPTER 3

"What the hell is this?" Xavier asked, slapping a pile of paper down on his desk with a disgusted sigh.

I blinked in confusion at the pages. I'd been so caught up in wondering if I still smelled like the sex, I'd gotten so close to having that I hadn't been paying attention to Xavier. I realized in an instant of absolute horror that he was talking about my manuscript and fought back the sudden urge to vomit right then and there. Tears sprang to my eyes and were about to fall when I saw the flash of amusement around his lips and made a strangled sound of disbelief. "Are you making fun of me?" I demanded, glaring at him with the mock outrage that had replaced the previous misery I'd felt. I grabbed the manuscript from his desk and blinked back tears. "You almost made me cry and I'm not a crier."

Xavier laughed. "Sorry, blame *schadenfreude*. I might get a perverse pleasure in seeing that moment of absolute panic in a student's eyes when I tell them their work is crap when it's actually really freaking good. That," he pointed at the first fifteen thousand words of my dystopian novel, "is really freaking good."

"Yeah?" I chewed on my bottom lip and considered my split desire to both graciously accept his praise of my writing and to run out of his office, manuscript in hand, and hide it away from the world so no one else could ever see it again.

My writing had always been so intensely private, except for schoolwork, that showing it to anyone, especially my super critical, super talented professor, was a fresh kind of torment. At the same time, if I was going to write, really write, I wanted to get better. It might hurt like hell but hearing the brutal truth from Xavier's lips would make me a stronger writer.

"Yeah, and if you're going to do this, you have to develop a much thicker skin, Elena. For Old One's sake, you dug a bullet out of me and fought your way across campus not six months ago. Buck up," he said with a twisted smile.

I nodded. "Okay, 'Buck up.' I'll put it on my to-do list." I picked up my phone and pretended to jot it down in my notes.

"Smart ass," Xavier muttered with a grin.

"Alright," I said, taking a deep breath. "Hit me with your feedback and don't hold back. I'm bucking up as of right now." I flipped the cover page and winced at the array of red ink notes.

"Well," he began, taking a sip from his coffee mug. "For starters, I think you need to switch from third person to first. I love your depth of description, but the story would be more immediate and accessible if you wrote it in first."

I chewed my lip as I scanned the page, rereading my own words. "I can try it," I said, musing over his suggestion. I thought of the shelf of books in my room and tried to remember which authors wrote in which style. It would be interesting to see what my favorite authors did.

He broke down his comments, explaining his thoughts with a patience I hadn't thought possible after my first few classes with him. He'd been a major part of me getting into AWA, or so I'd thought when I was under the assumption I was here because of a scholarship and not actually because I was the heir to the Russian Alphaship.

I'd expected his class to be the one place I'd feel welcome, which was why it had hit so hard that he'd immediately torn into every single piece I'd passed in. I'd been alone, completely out of place in a world I didn't understand or even like, and the man I'd hoped would be my mentor had been a huge dick.

We'd made peace after I'd saved his life and he'd explained that his pissy attitude was based primarily on his being in the midst of a brutal divorce and custody battle with his ex over their daughter.

He'd approached me about working on a novel right after the plane crash. I'd known it was an attempt to pry my focus away from yet another tragedy, but I'd taken it anyway. Writing was a way to escape, a way to create a world I'd rather live in than the one dogging my every step.

I blinked when I heard my name repeated with a question after it.

"Elena?" Xavier arched an eyebrow and shook his head. "I think maybe we'll leave off here. Give the first person a chance and we'll meet back next week. Okay?"

I nodded slowly, feeling as if I'd just been dragged out of a fugue state. "Yeah, yeah, sorry. I drifted off. Early training session."

Xavier leveled his gaze on me and quirked a knowing smile. "Go, or you'll be late for class."

I picked up the manuscript and rolled it as I stood, fidgeting nervously as I searched for the balls to ask the one question that had been playing on my mind these last few months.

"Just spit it out, Elena," Xavier said with an edge of impatience that made me swallow my fear and blurt.

"It's not derivative, is it?" I shifted, tightening my grip on the paper. "I know dystopian exploded in young adult back when Collins released, but it's been around forever. Atwood, Orwell, Burgess, I mean they all created their own version of a world in ruin." I chewed my lip and blew out a deep breath. "Am I regurgitating or creating?"

Xavier's dark eyes narrowed as he watched me suffer in the silence that fell after my question. His inhalation sounded like the roar of the Atlantic waves I'd grown up with, it was half deafening and too loaded with importance for a simple breath.

"Do you need me to validate you?" He kept his voice low, almost a murmur that I'd have had to struggle to hear if I hadn't been a wolf.

I thought about it for a second then nodded sharply. "Yes. Fuck yes." A blush flared to life, heating my cheeks. "Sorry."

"Don't apologize and don't question your right to create something similar or completely different than what's already created." He pushed to his feet and leaned forward, resting his hands on the desk. "This is your first book. Just get it out."

I nodded but inside my chest was tight with nerves and doubt. I hoped that just meant I was a real author, since it was my understanding all creative types were self-deprecating anxiety ridden children at heart. "Thanks," I mumbled, turning for the door.

"Elena," Xavier interrupted my deep-seated angst as I stepped through his doorway. "Do you trust me?"

I answered automatically. "Yes."

"Then trust me on this. One day, your name will be synonymous with Atwood, Orwell, Burgess, and more. You've got a remarkable way with words, kid." He sank back into his seat and turned his attention to a stack of papers, finished with his validation of me.

My lips lifted in a smile that reached my soul and filled me with a feeling of lightness. I floated down the hallway with my manuscript pressed to my chest, not caring that I looked like an utter fool.

♀ ♀ ♀

"It's too hot for pants," Rory complained, throwing the pair of jeans she'd just tried on and taken off onto the growing pile of rejects.

"It's hot now, but it'll be cooler tonight. Wear the blue pants," I murmured, turning the page of the novel I'd grabbed from her shelf, which was almost as impressive as my own. "With the white shirt and gold earrings."

Rory mumbled something under her breath and disappeared into the bathroom with a huff. I lifted my head out of the book and raised my eyebrows. I'd known her for almost a full school year now and I'd yet to see her stomp around like a petulant child. Something was wrong.

"Hey," I said, putting the book down and sliding off her bed. I moved to the door of the bathroom and watched as she fussed with her hair even though it looked perfect. "What's up with you? You're all…" I waved a hand in front of me and searched for the right word. I settled on, "weird."

Rory glared at me in the mirror. "I can't be weird every once in a while?" Her tone was clipped, which was more surprising than the bad mood. I pushed down the hurt of being snapped at and laid a hand on her arm.

"What's wrong? Talk to me."

Her gaze dropped and her jaw tightened. For a moment, I thought she was going to throw me off and finish her snit in private, but then she lifted eyes filled with misery and sagged.

"It's all falling apart," her voice broke with emotion that struck me by surprise. I'd seen my friend pissed off plenty of times, but never near tears. I pulled her into my arms for a hug and held on even tighter when she started to cry.

I found her robe on the back of the bathroom door and waited while she pulled it on and belted it in a knot. "Come on," I touched her gently, steering her towards the oversized lounge chair set into the corner by her bookshelf. When she sank into the deep cushions, looking for the world like a porcelain doll about to break. My stomach churned as I sat on the edge of the bed and waited for her to speak.

"I see the way you and Bash are around each other," Rory said in a small voice. She didn't look at me when she spoke and, instead, focused on peeling off the remains of her navy-blue nail polish. "Even with the shit between you two since the Connor fiasco, there's still a bond between you that anyone with half a brain can see."

"It's the mate bond," I said, wondering where she was going with this.

"Exactly. It's something real and," she chewed on her lip, "not measurable, but perceivable." Rory lifted her gaze and I saw deep grief and confusion in her dark eyes. "Darius and I," she swallowed hard and squeezed her eyes shut for a moment. A tear leaked from the inner corner and traced down her cheek. "He's not my mate, Elena."

I shook my head immediately. "No, Rory, you can't judge your relationship on mine and Bash's. Besides," I quickly did the math in my head, "our bond didn't even solidify until we were together almost six months. It's different for everyone. Even Katherine told me that she and Quinn didn't bond right away and they're the epitome of relationship goals."

Rory wiped her face with the back of her hand and sniffed. "It's not the same. I don't know how to explain it, I just know. I'm in love with Darius, but it's never going to happen for us. He's not my mate."

My heart sunk for her as memories of love without that all-important bond resurfaced for the millionth time lately. I'd loved Connor with the innocence that you only give a first love and he'd crushed me. If it weren't for this soul-deep mysterious bond between Bash and I, I didn't know if I'd be able to love him with the same abandon.

Even before the bond had somehow magically become this tangible thing between us, I'd known. A part of my soul had leaped from me and into him the moment we'd crashed into one another outside the auditorium on my first day at AWA. I'd looked into his emerald eyes and had sunk.

I didn't know what to say to help Rory through this. I'd questioned the reality of soulmates my entire life until I'd literally bumped headfirst into mine, but I knew she'd always believed. Her parents were soulmates and there was no way she'd settle for anything less.

I knew now was not the time to tell her about the new layer of connection between me and Bash. It would only make this worse. So, I did the only thing I knew how to do and crawled into the chair with her.

"You're a giant," Rory mumbled as I settled in beside her, smushing her for a moment.

"You love it," I said with a grin and wrapped my arm around her shoulders. I'd never truly been a girly girl, but I'd sat with Sara and Bethany through more than one dramatic heart break and they'd helped me through mine. Just being there for her and listening would help the most.

She curled into me once I'd folded my long legs into the chair. "I've been waiting and praying for something to shift between us, but it hasn't happened. I love him, I adore him, but there's something missing. I can feel it in here," she touched her chest and rubbed. "Like an emptiness."

I nodded slowly and measured my response, not wanting to say the wrong thing. If she decided to stay with Darius, even without the bond, and I said something negative about him, she'd always remember that.

"What do you want to do?" I asked, figuring simple questions were safe.

Rory sighed and it rolled through her like a wave of grief. I felt it as surely as I felt her petite frame nestled up against me. "I've been going over it again and again, and I think," her voice broke on a sob, "I think we need to break up."

My eyebrows lifted in surprise and shame. She'd been dealing with this while I was off on spring vacation, and I'd had no idea. I bit down on my lip and ignored the guilt building in my chest. This was about her feelings, not mine. Still, I needed her to know I was sorry. "I'm so sorry you had to go through this alone. I've been caught up in my head and should have realized you were going through something."

She shifted her head and smiled up at me. "I kept it pretty close to the chest but it's just getting too big to ignore anymore. I can barely sleep. I just don't think it's fair, to him or me, to stay together when we're not fated." She squeezed her eyes shut again and looked away.

"Oh, Rory," I pulled her in closer and hugged tightly until she wheezed for breath and struggled to be let free. I didn't let her free. Instead, I pressed a loud kiss to the top of her head. "I'm here, all the time, and I love you." The words of friendship that I'd only ever said to Sara and

Bethany flowed straight from my heart. They felt right. I might not have known Rory from birth, but she was as much a part of my heart as my family and best friends.

Her lips quirked and her eyelids lifted to reveal dark eyes shiny with tears. "I love you, too, weirdo," she murmured then rested her head in the crook of my arm and sighed. "I don't think I should go to the party. I'm a mess and need to talk to Darius before I can show my face."

"Is he going to be there?" I asked.

"No, he's still not back from his parent's place."

I rubbed her arm and shifted my body until I got enough traction to pull myself out of the chair. When I reached back and pulled Rory to her feet, she grumbled, "What are you doing?"

"I'm getting you dressed and ready for the party," I said with a grin. Before she could flop back in the chair, I placed the blue pants and white shirt in her arms and pointed to the bathroom. "Go. Get ready and have a fun night with me, no boys, no expectations, no heartbreak. Let's drink and dance until we're exhausted and come back here to eat Cheetos and pass out."

She stared blankly at me for a moment before the corners of her mouth quirked up and a familiar light lit her dark eyes. "Yeah," she nodded and bounced a little, grinning now. I could still see the strain of emotion hiding just behind the light, but it was dimmer now. "That sounds perfect." Rory threw her arms around me and squeezed then disappeared into the bathroom humming a top forty song about feeling good as hell.

I sat down on the edge of the bed and picked up my

phone to text Bash. After our little sexually charged interlude earlier, we were both looking forward to spending the night together. But, as much as I wanted to rip his clothes off with my teeth and bite him all over his delectable body, my girl needed me, and raging hormones could wait. We had the rest of our lives together, after all. My fingers flew across the keys.

Hey, so Rory's in a bit of a funk and needs a girl's night tonight. Party's still on but she's my date. Think you'll recover from the shock and loss?

I grinned as I hit send and he started typing back immediately.

If my balls get any bluer, they're going to fall off and then where will we be? The fate of our future children depends on what you do next.

I snorted as amused tears wet my eyes and my heart stretched a fraction more for my mate. Then his words sunk in and a wave of warmth flowed over me. Our future children. I typed my response quickly.

Consider tonight a lesson in tantric foreplay, then. Pain is pleasure, or so I've heard.

I pressed my legs together and thought about his hands on me earlier, his mouth pressed between my thighs. "Fuck," I murmured to myself, wondering if I'd be able to make it through the party.

What about bros before hos? :(

My laughter echoed through the room, startlingly loud. Rory pulled the bathroom door open and stuck her head out. "You say something?"

"No, just laughing at something Bash texted." I eyed her smokey liner and nodded in approval. "Love the eyes."

Rory beamed and went back to getting ready. I turned back to my sexy text wars.

Sorry. Tonight, it's sisters before misters. And if Rory finds out you called her a ho, she's going to destroy you. Xoxo

I hit send just as the bathroom door opened again and Rory darted out to root through her closet. "I'm not in the mood for that outfit," she mumbled, pushing hangers aside. With a triumphant cheer, she pulled something long and black from her closet and disappeared back into the bathroom, calling over her shoulder, "I won't be much longer."

It had been a good idea, girl's night, even if it meant I was left with an uncomfortable pressure between my legs and Bash's balls were as blue as my eyes.

The bathroom door opened slowly, and Rory stepped out, shocking every uncomfortable thought out of my mind and leaving me gaping. She grinned at my expression and did a full turn with hands on hips to give me the full effect.

She wore a black one piece that was tight on her petite frame, highlighting every curve she had to perfection. The halter top was barely there in the front, cutting deep between her breasts, almost to her navel, and non-existent in the back. As I sat, stunned, and wondering if I could pull off something like that, she bent and pulled on black wedge booties that finished the look to perfection.

When she looked up, Rory's eyes were lit with fire and a determination I hadn't seen in a while. Her lips turned up in a saucy grin that made me laugh.

"Well, what are you waiting for?" she asked, cocking an eyebrow. "Let's go get into trouble."

CHAPTER 4

"I might die from frostbite tonight, but at least I'll look good when I meet the Old Ones," Rory said with a happy grin as we picked our way through the forest surrounding Alpha Wolf Academy.

The moon was just a sliver in the night sky, giving the shadows around us an ominous depth. Our lupine eyes saw more than a human could, but that darkness was so nearly complete that it made me a little antsy. I glanced nervously at the long shadows and saw Viktor behind every tree.

"So, I never asked since I was kind of wrapped up in my own misery," Rory reached out a hand and touched my arm. "Did you and Bash get a chance to talk yet?"

I pulled my attention back from the spooky forest and blinked. I'd been complaining to her just last night that Bash had been avoiding me for too long and that I would track him down and force him to talk today if I had to sit on him. It felt like a lifetime had passed since Bash and I had touched one another's minds, but it had been just a few hours ago.

The silence stretched out between us until it became too obvious to ignore. "Why are you being weird?" Rory asked with furrowed brows.

"It's my turn," I mumbled, not really wanting to tell her in case it ruined her good mood but not wanting to lie, either.

She chuckled. "Touché, asshole. Now tell me what's up."

She was a bossy little wench, I thought. Good thing I loved her.

"We talked this morning." I started the confession slowly, working up to the real news. Part of me wanted to hold it back, not for Rory, but because it was so special, so new, that I wanted to hold it like a promise, close to my heart for just Bash and I. But she was my girl, so I spilled the beans. "It wasn't going well, at first. Bash was upset that I didn't tell him about me and Connor, and he's totally right to be mad," I said in a rush when Rory opened her mouth to comment. I knew she was of the opinion that I'd made a giant oops in that situation.

She snapped her mouth shut and just kept walking. Since I knew she was dying to ask me what happened, I finished the story.

"I was trying to push my emotions into him, to share how sorry I am and how afraid, and then," I smiled remembering it and ran a hand through my hair. "Then he heard my thoughts."

"Huh?" Rory came to an abrupt stop and tugged my arm until I turned to face her in the dim light. Her eyes, always wide, were wider than usual and as dark as the shadows that still concerned me. "What do you mean? Like, heard you, heard you?"

I nodded, still not sure my brain fully accepted what had happened. My heart did, though, I realized, and so did my soul. It had practically leaped when I'd heard his whispered question in my mind.

"Yeah, I heard his thoughts and he heard mine." I arched an eyebrow and grinned wickedly. "His thoughts are disgusting, by the way."

Rory's arms wrapped around me a second later and squeezed the air from my lungs. "I've heard of that happening, but I've never known anyone who had it. I'm so fucking happy for you guys." She buried her face in my jacket and just held me for a long moment. I wondered if it was to hide tears and give herself a moment.

I gave her the time she needed then turned away and kept walking, figuring if she was tearing up, I would just make it worse by noticing.

"I've decided to use this new power to bring Sebastian Reeves to his knees, of course," I said glibly, waving a hand in the air as if he were just one boy toy of many.

"Of course," Rory agreed, catching up to me. "He might have his own tricks, though. So, you better watch out."

I thought of the pressure between my legs that hadn't quite gone away since this morning and sighed. "Old Ones, I hope so."

I could hear the music now, blasting from speakers to fill the surrounding woods with sexy, casual, cheer. The students at AWA held regular parties in the same clearing for the same occasions for as long as anyone could remember. The staff ignored the gatherings. We were all over twenty, after all. Wolves started school later than humans. We took extra years at home with family to learn our place in the pack.

Fairy lights had been strung around the clearing and were hooked up to a generator that sat tucked into the trees, barely making a sound. A makeshift bar was set up at one end of what would be a meadow once the grass started growing again. It was stocked with every kind of alcohol known to man, only high end, of course. Several kegs had been tapped already and were in full swing. It was amazing what you could do when your family had endless amounts of money and influence. I had no first-hand knowledge of such behavior.

I felt Bash before I saw him. His thoughts and emotions were like a warm embrace at the back of my mind, teasing me into turning to catch his gaze. His smile was knowing and a little frustrated, which made me bite back a laugh.

I'll agree to play fair if you do, too. I murmured through our bond.

He nodded, just the barest movement of his head, never moving his gaze from mine. The light of the bonfire flashed in his eyes, making the emerald green dance. My heart swelled with love for him, so thick and heavy it ached.

He swallowed and closed his eyes for a moment as a rush of emotion took him over. *I love you.* He thought the words and felt them, and the enormity of it was staggering.

"Drinks!" Rory reached out and grabbed my hand

without looking and dragged me toward the bar and away from Bash. He shot me a half grin and a shrug and turned back to his friends.

Rory's hips swayed as she mixed two white Russians, heavy on the Russian, light on the white. I eyed the cup for a moment and told myself it wasn't going to attack. Not all Russians were bad. I had to come to terms with that if I was ever going to vie for my rightful place in the Russian pack.

It was sweet with the sting of vodka and I drank it quickly under Rory's watchful eye. There was no point sipping booze as wolves, our metabolisms were too quick, even at our age, to allow us to get drunk on limited alcohol. I'd rarely been truly drunk in my twenty-two years, but I was primed to get there tonight. With a grin, I finished my drink and slammed the plastic cup down on the bar top.

"Another, bar wench!" I demanded with a laugh.

"I'll bar wench you," Rory replied. She danced her fingers over various bottles of liquor and stopped on a short rounded bottle.

"No." I stepped back, eyes wide and hands help up.

"Yes." Rory nabbed the bottle of Patrón and two shot glasses, then darted away without looking to see if I was following. I did, swaying my own hips to the music pouring out of the speakers.

By my sixth shot, I felt pretty good. Whenever I moved my head quickly, the world seemed to blur in a magical way. I dipped my head and closed my eyes, undulating my body to the beat of the latest hits.

"We need to go to Greece!" Rory said with a giggle. "I

want to lie in the sun." She leaned forward and whispered, "nude."

Her eyes were soft and so pretty, I thought as I shook my head and gripped her arm. "No." I shook my head, liking the way it made me float. "We can't leave, or you know who will find me and…" I lifted my thumb to my neck and mimed slitting my throat.

"Shhh," Rory pressed a finger to her lips and leaned so close I felt her lips on my ear. "Voldemort might hear you."

We burst into giggles. I wrapped my arms around her and hugged, feeling overcome with love for her. "I love you, do you know that?" I asked, slurring my words.

She nodded, eyes wide. "I do. I feel it in here." She pointed to her boob.

"Das your boob," I said chuckling. "I like your boobs, too."

"Awww," she said, nodding as if I'd said something wise, which I was pretty sure was true. "Thank you. You have great boobs, too." She reached out and cupped my breast. "They're so perky." She smiled crookedly and grabbed her own chest. "Mine are too small."

I shook my head adamantly. "That's not true at all. Your boobs are perfect. Aren't her boobs perfect?" I asked a guy I kind of recognized who just happened to be walking.

He grinned enthusiastically and said, "Yeah, they are!" making Rory turn bright pink. When the guy stumbled as he turned away, we burst into teary laughter and clutched at each other's arms for support.

"Old Ones," Rory held up the near empty bottle of

tequila. "I think I'm drunk." She frowned and looked around the clearing then nodded. "Yup, I'm drunk! Are you drunk, too?" She stared at me as if she'd be able to tell just by looking.

I nodded slowly, suddenly not liking the way my head felt when I moved. "I'm spinning," I murmured as I searched out the solid trunk of the tree we were sitting on. I set my feet firmly on the ground and held onto the rough bark and felt the world right itself. "I might need to stop for a bit."

"Pfft!" Rory made a dismissive gesture and stood up. She swayed for a moment before extending a hand. "Come on. Time to dance!"

When I didn't automatically take her hand, she reached down and grabbed mine. The moment my hand left the tree trunk, my world began to spin again. I wobbled and threw out my hands.

"Okay," Rory said with another giggle. "You sit here and rest. I'll find Bash for you." She looked out at the people dancing around the bonfire. "And maybe dance a bit. Bye." She elongated the final "e" as she danced away.

I blinked after her, wondering how I was going to move ever again. A laugh bubbled up and slipped through my lips at the thought. The sound of my laugh, so loud inside my head, startled me. My heart pounded violently in my chest, slamming into my ribs so that it felt like a marching band was alive and competing for gold inside me. I grasped at my jacket and tugged it away from my skin as panic began to rise from my gut into my throat.

"Hey." Bash appeared out of nowhere and knelt in front of me. "Hey, look at me. That's right. Breathe." He reached out and took my fingers, unfurling them from my chest and placing them firmly back on the stump. "There, feel that? You're not going anywhere."

I stared at him in wonder. "How?" I couldn't seem to finish the question with words. My mind swam with unintelligible thoughts and emotions.

"I felt you," he explained, moving to take Rory's abandoned seat. "Here." He handed me a bottle of water. "Drink it all and you'll start feeling better in no time."

I obeyed because it was the only thing I could do. Free choice or thought was out of the question for the next little while, at least. My eyelids fluttered shut for a moment, then popped back open when that set my world sharply on its axis again. "Whoa!" I exclaimed with a chuckle. "Did you feel that?"

Bash nodded and reached up to brush his thumb over my cheek. "Yeah, I felt it."

His hand felt nice on my skin, so I leaned into his palm and hummed contentedly. "I love you," I murmured, turning my face to inhale his scent. "You're so good to me. Connor wasn't good to me. No, he hurt me so bad. In here." I lifted my other hand to my heart and tapped.

Words tumbled from my lips like frothy water over a waterfall. It felt so good to finally be able to talk about it with Bash, with the man I loved. I smiled into his palm and spilled my heart at his feet.

"I thought I knew what love was, did you know that?" I lifted my head to look into his emerald depths. "I love your eyes."

Bash watched me intently, focused only on me. It was amazing being the center of his world, but he was the center of mine, so it was right. My head flopped forward, too heavy to stay up, and he gathered me into his arms.

"I like it here," I murmured softly with a sleepy smile. "You smell good, and look good, and you're really good at sex." My brain lit up as I remembered our interlude early. "Remember that thing you did to me this morning?" When he didn't respond immediately, I started to recap and felt his chest began to rise and fall. "Are you laughing at me?"

"Oh, Elena," Bash's voice rumbled through his chest into my heart. "You are without a doubt the most amazing woman I've ever met. My world shifted when you walked into me."

I made a dismissive sound. "You mean when you bumped into me and gave me a concussion?" I giggled, remembering the way he'd looked through my knocked head.

"Yeah," he brushed a hand over my hair. "So," he said slowly, tilting my face up to look at him. "I don't need to worry about Connor?"

My eyes went wide, and I shook my head, pulling back to stare at him. "No," I said, then heard my own voice echo too loudly in my head. "He's just Connor, but you're *you*." I nodded because that explained exactly what I was feeling. There was no comparison for me.

He looked at me, into me, eyes narrowing just the tiniest bit. I let my hand float up to his gorgeous face to trace the sharp lines of his jaw, the stubble on his cheek, delectable curve of his full lips. My eyes focused in on those lips now.

I nibbled them. I couldn't help it, it was inevitable.

They were the most perfect lips in existence, and they were mine.

"Mine," I murmured like a purr against his mouth. His lips turned up in a smile.

"We should get you moving around a little," Bash said, pulling those lips away as he tugged me to my feet.

I swayed and laughed with pure joy when I tilted forward into his strong arms. "Whoops!" I giggled and wrapped my arms around his neck. "Guess you'll just have to hold me up." I shot him my sexiest bedroom eyes then blinked wildly when an eyelash blurred my vision. "Ow."

Bash's hands moved to my shoulders and righted me. "Here," he said softly, using his forefinger and thumb to widen my eyes slightly. He leaned in and puffed a breath of air straight into my eye before I realized what was happening.

"Ughhh," I wrenched back and stumbled but caught myself on a tree. I blinked rapidly, trying to wet my now dry eye, and realized the intrusive eyelash was no longer there. "Oh," I said, wiping rogue tears from my cheek. "Thanks."

"You, my dear, are soused." Bash pulled me into his side and wrapped his arm around my shoulders, making me feel safe and petite. For someone who'd been 5'10" tall since my tenth birthday, that was a pretty impressive feat, so I snuggled deeper into his embrace and enjoyed it as we strolled around the field.

We'd stopped briefly to chat with several groups of Bash's friends when something interesting caught my attention. My head had stopped spinning sometime around the second lap of the party, so it was easier to focus now.

"Who's that?" I asked, nudging Bash to get his attention. Subtly or, what I hoped was subtly, I nodded toward the far end of the field where a group of students were dancing. Rory had her head thrown back and her arms in the air and was undulating in a very Dirty Dancing type move that had my eyebrow quirking up.

I'd never seen her dance that way before, even with Darius, even in the few other times we'd imbibed too much and gotten wild. If I didn't know better, I'd have thought she was flirting.

"Who are we talking about?" Bash asked, turning to follow the direction I was staring.

I suddenly remembered with startling clarity that Darius was one of Bash's best friends and that Rory was supposed to be madly in love with him. I shot out a hand, cupped his chin, and surged forward with a kiss meant to wipe any and all questions from his mind.

It worked. His body moved closer and his hands clutched at my clothes, trying to grab more. I poured every ounce of lust I'd felt all day long into the kiss, losing myself in the process, and came up gasping for air a minute later.

Bash gaped down at me as his chest rose and fell. "Old Ones," he muttered, swiping a hand through his hair. "You're feeling better."

I smirked, feeling the raw feminine power my sex had mastered ages ago. "I'd feel a hell of a lot better if..." my words stopped dead in my throat, and I felt the blood drain from my face.

"Elena?" Bash grasped my arms and looked around wildly. "What's wrong?"

I couldn't speak. All I could do was stare into the face of the girl I'd let die on the ice in the middle of a frozen pond in the Idaho wilderness.

The girl Rory was dancing with was supposed to be dead.

CHAPTER 5

Adeline?

A bitter taste filled my mouth as I stared, unable to break my gaze from the girl's fall of dark hair or the beautiful copper skin that made her look kissed by the moon. She'd have dark eyes, I knew, eyes that had gone glassy and blank as I'd raced away from her bleeding body.

I squeezed my eyes shut, praying it was just a nightmare. "You're not real," I murmured, taking shaky breaths in, and letting them out in a deliberately slow push. "You're not real. I'm alright. You're not real." I opened my eyes and bit back a cry of grief.

"Elena," Bash turned my head to face him, forcing me to break my gaze and look at him. "What's happening? Talk to me. It's all jumbled in there." His fingertips grazed my forehead then moved down to press over my heart. "Who's not real."

I stared up at him. He was real, I told myself. Bash was

here and real and mine. The ground beneath my feet was real. The chill of the night air on my skin was real. Whoever Rory was dancing with, it wasn't Adeline; she was dead.

I steeled myself and looked again.

Adeline swayed to the music, rocking her hips side to side as Rory moved around her, eyes closed, completely oblivious to the fact that she was dancing with a ghost. My throat went painfully dry as I watched and waited for the world to right itself, but it didn't.

"That's Adeline," I whispered, leaning into Bash because my legs felt as if they wouldn't hold my weight much longer.

"Who?" Bash looked across the field and saw them. His body stiffened as he saw Rory, saw the look on her face, the way she moved closer to my ghost, and understood. "What…" he trailed off as he realized who she was with. "Holy fuck." His eyes went wide. "No," Bash turned and took my shoulders. "Elena, no, that's not Adeline. Look at me."

I looked at him. His face blurred for a moment then went back to normal.

"That's not Adeline," he repeated. Bash reached for my hand and gripped it tight. "She's gone."

"Then who is she?" I said on a breathy gasp, trying to focus on his reassurance. He'd known Adeline, had taken classes with her, and he knew exactly what had happened out on the ice over Winter break.

"I don't know," he admitted and tugged me into his arms. "Let's go find out."

I nodded, knowing the nightmare wouldn't end if I

didn't face it head on. "Okay." I stepped forward then stopped and looked up at him. "Don't give Rory a hard time. She and Darius are..." I trailed off, not wanting to say too much but needing to defend my girl.

His jaw clenched and, for a moment, I thought he'd take up Darius' side right here and now. He was fiercely loyal to his friends and family; it was one of the things that I loved most about him. He took a steadying breath and unclenched his jaw. "Okay," he murmured, nodding sharply. "But you know this is going to crush him."

"I know," I said with a sigh. "It's hurting her, too."

"Doesn't look like it," he grumbled.

I looked and had to admit that Bash was right. Rory was glowing. She was undulating to the rhythm of the music, her smile radiant, her gaze locked on the ghost of Adeline.

She looked infatuated.

I swallowed and hoped my bestie knew what she was doing.

Bash linked his hand through mine as we crossed the field. I leaned on him even though I felt a lot steadier now. Although, the closer we got to the girl, the more my knees trembled and the more his grasp tightened.

Adeline's ghost noticed us first and stopped moving, stopped looking at Rory, stopped breathing. Our gazes met and recognition flared.

"Elena?" Her voice came out breathy and unsteady.

I recognized it immediately and gasped out, "Adeline?"

She blinked, long and slow, and I saw grief flood her dark eyes as she glanced away.

Rory twirled and grinned at me then noticed Bash and

ground to a halt. Her lips fell open and she looked as if she were about to start apologizing, but then something shifted in her eyes and she snapped her lips shut. She turned away from his judgmental glare and looked back and forth between me and her dance partner. "Hey! Elena, this is Addison. Addison, this is my best friend, Elena."

"I know who she is," the girl said softly in a whisper that was almost drowned out by the music.

Rory frowned and looked back and forth again, her eyes narrowing as she felt the tension between us. "What's going on? Do you guys know each other?"

Her name raced over and over through my mind. Addison. Addison. Not Adeline. Addison. I couldn't seem to break my gaze away from hers.

"Adeline was my sister," the girl said, louder this time.

"What?" Rory shook her head, obviously trying to piece it all together. "Adeline, as in..." her head twisted sharply towards me. "Adeline from the crash?" Her hand shot out and grabbed my forearm as realization dawned across her face. Her previously radiant flush paled now as she turned to look at Addison.

No one spoke and the tension grew as seconds ticked by. Finally, unable to stand it anymore, I gestured towards the woods. "Let's go talk, in private."

Bash stayed by my side as we left the crowd and moved into the quiet provided by the thick evergreens. His fingers squeezed mine and through our bond he sent reassurances that helped my muscles relax.

When we'd cleared the party and the music, I stopped and turned to face Addison. She stood apart from us and looked unsure. Rory stood in the middle, her body language torn between the girl she'd just met and me. I frowned and took in the flush that was back on her cheeks, the way her fingers fluttered as she tried to keep her hands by her sides. Everything about her seemed to want to go to Addison. It was like she needed to touch her to settle.

My eyes went wide and darted between Rory and Addison as wonder filled my chest with aching for them both, but I held my thoughts back in case I was wrong. Besides, I thought, lifting my gaze to Addison, it wasn't exactly a great time to ask my best friend if she'd just found her soul mate.

"Adeline didn't say anything about having a sister," I said, taking in every detail of her face and form. If there was a difference between them, I didn't see it. "Are you twins?"

Addison shook her head then lifted her gaze upward, blinking several times to clear the sheen of tears from her eyes. "No," she said, sniffing, when she got herself under control. "She's my big sister." She closed her eyes and whispered, "Was my big sister."

A lump formed in my throat and pushed like jagged ice against my windpipe, making it hard to fill my lungs. A flash of memory, of Adeline's body lying on the snow with her life blood spreading out as I raced away, unable to save her, filled my mind. Bash inched closer and squeezed my hand to ground me.

"I was there," the words stumbled from my lips before I thought to say them. It was the truth, wasn't it? I was there when Adeline died, when one of Viktor's mercenaries shot her from the tree line because I'd led us out into the open, thinking we'd had enough of a lead to be safe. "It was my fault…" I let the words hang between us and lowered my gaze, ashamed to look her in the eye.

"No, it wasn't," Addison said sharply, wrenching my gaze from the ground to her face. "Ms. Morgan told me everything." Her hand darted out and grabbed my forearm tightly. "She said you'd take the blame. She said you'd try to shoulder everything. I can see she's right." Addison shook her head and pity flooded her dark eyes. "Elena, it's not your fault. None of this is your fault."

The urge to spill my guts at her feet, to admit my culpability in all of this, my connection to the psychopath that had brought all of this shit to our doorstep, nearly overwhelmed me. I opened my mouth and the words formed of their own volition, shoving to the tip of my tongue.

Then Rory was there, stepping forward and linking her hand with the one not held by Bash. I glanced at her and offered an uncertain smile. Her look of reassurance and trust made my chest ache. I squeezed my eyes shut and let the tears come.

"I'm so sorry," I whispered through uneven breaths. "We thought we were safe. We thought…" I shook my head, unable to explain.

My head swam with confusion. I didn't know how much of the story had been shared with Addison, how much she knew of what had brought down the plane. She'd talked to Ms. Morgan, she'd said, but that didn't mean she was on the inside of this unstable, life-destroying secret that was tearing me and my friends apart.

Addison stepped forward and reached forward. Without hesitation, I released Rory's and Bash's hands and took hers. They were always there for me when I needed their strength. It was the least I could do to offer Adeline's sister the same.

I took her into my arms and felt the strength of her. Like her sister, she was tall and willowy, but looks were apparently deceiving. She was strong, of body and mind, from what I was sensing, and she would be alright. I felt her strength move through our combined limbs into me, like a wave of forgiveness for Adeline's death. With every ounce of relief in me, I grabbed on and let the hope wash the darkness away.

There was so much darkness in me now, I thought, releasing her with a soft smile. For a girl who'd grown up on the banks of Newfoundland, in the sun and saltwater air, I'd come a long way… down. I knew many would say the opposite, that my newly revealed circumstances meant I'd come up in the world. After all, I was a part of The Sisterhood now, a friend and ally of the Alpha family, a student at Alpha Wolf Academy. I was a far cry from the Elena I'd always known and that was terrifying.

"She seemed nice," Bash murmured as we watched Rory and Addison stroll away. His eyes narrowed as Rory's hand skimmed against Addison's and their fingers linked. A low growl started in his chest and rumbled out.

I swiveled to stand in front of him and planted a palm over his chest, feeling the vibrations of anger and frustration there. I knew that all he could see was betrayal of his best friend, not the pain behind the scenes, so I stayed calm and kept my voice pitched low. "Calm your wolf," I said, raising my other hand to his cheek to draw his gaze down. When he looked down at me, I saw the flickers of wildness in his emerald eyes and swallowed down a surprising wave of lust.

Inappropriate given what just happened, I berated myself silently.

"Bash," I said, focusing his attention. "Do me a favor, will you? Look at them." I gestured towards the two girls, who couldn't keep their eyes off each other. "What do you see?"

He grumbled something unintelligible then muttered, "They look happy." He looked down at me with a frown. "She's cheating on Darius. How am I supposed to be okay with this?"

I shook my head. "You're not and he won't be either, none of them will, but just look." I took his jaw in my hand and turned his head. "Watch their body language. What do you see?" I held my breath, hoping someone who'd experienced the miracle of the mate bond would be able to see it in others.

His whoosh of breath told me he'd seen and understood the implications. "Fuck," Bash growled, but there was no avarice in this sound, just pained understanding. "This is going to destroy him."

I laid my head on his chest and closed my eyes, wishing I could spare Darius this pain while basking in joy for my best friend. "Be there for him like you always are and it'll get better in time. Hopefully, he'll find his mate soon." But I didn't have much real hope of that. It was rare to find your mate at our age, rarer still to find a same-sex mate. That Bash and I, and now Rory and Addison had found our other halves, didn't bode well statistically for Darius. Some wolves waited hundreds of years to find their mates. Katherine had said once that it only made the bond sweeter to wait so long and then find your soul.

I thanked the Old Ones I'd already found mine and that he was so fucking sexy.

His arms came around me, loosely, comforting, but that shock of lust I'd felt earlier reared its head again and burned through me. I bit down on my lips to hold it back. This wasn't the time or place to get horny.

Bash's body stiffened and his arms tightened, pulling me in closer. I heard his inhale, deep and knowing, and lost my battle on control as his hips shifted forward, giving me a hint of his response.

My fingers found his and tugged as I slipped out of his embrace and headed farther into the woods. They weren't shadowed and spooky anymore; I barely even registered the night. Excitement and need danced over my skin, under my skin, and through my soul as we picked up speed and raced into the forest.

The cool night air whipped my hair back as we ran, hand in hand, jumping over logs and bushes, skirting around thick groves of evergreens. The sound of his delighted laughter, bubbling out of his chest, made me soar with unbridled joy.

When his arm went taut and snapped me back into his arms, I let that joy free and threw back my head, trusting Bash to hold me up as I threw out my arms and dipped.

He held me steady, then pulled me up and fitted his mouth to mine in a kiss that claimed me anew. My hands lifted and dove into his thick dark hair to tug him even closer.

His lips moved from mine, branding every inch of skin they touched, lighting fires as they danced lower, down my throat and over my shoulder. He pushed at my jacket, pulling it down my arms, then fit his teeth over the curve of my neck and bit.

Hard.

I cried out and raked my nails over his neck, nearly collapsing at the rush of pained pleasure. Desperate need flooded my mind, spurring my hands to tear at clothes that hid skin.

Bursts of desire swamped me in flickers of sensation. His hands hot on my skin, the taste of him on my lips, blinding pleasure that nearly stole my breath.

When he dragged me to the mossy ground, covered in our discarded clothes, I slid over him, pushing him down to straddle his thighs. And when I rose up onto my knees, surrounding him, then sunk down, taking him into me, his roar of pleasure and gripped fingers on my hips, sang in my soul.

A brilliant burst of white light exploded behind my eyes when he lifted my hips and pulled them down to meet his thrust. We set a frantic pace, our bodies meeting with slaps of skin on skin and urgent calls for more. I squeezed my eyes shut and threw back my head, letting myself feel every sensation like a wave crashing into me.

My release built, so fast and furious that I barely had time to hang on before my body was clenching around

Bash, tightening in vicious spasms that dragged him over the precipice with me and sent us both flying.

I collapsed in a heap of slick naked flesh atop his chest and dragged in ragged breaths to steady my racing heart. When I could see again, I lifted my head and grinned at him. "That was super inappropriate."

His chuckle shook our combined bodies. "You started it." He pulled me back down and rolled us both to the side.

I rested my head on his arm and looked up at the dark sky above us. The stars stood out so clearly, it felt for a moment as if I were home. I smiled lazily and closed my eyes.

I felt the wave of awareness a second later and sat up, pushing my way out of Bash's embrace with adrenaline pumping through my heart so intensely, it felt like my chest couldn't possibly contain it.

"What's wrong?" Bash leaped up, his eyes wide with panic. He peered into the shadows, all senses on alert as he crouched, teeth bared, and hands raised to protect us both.

I pressed one hand to my throat and the other to my thundering chest and sucked in deep breaths meant to focus my mind as my skin crawled under the sensation of being watched. "Someone's here," I whispered, climbing to my feet. "Someone's watching us." I swallowed the acrid fear burning in my throat and yelled into the trees, "I know you're there! Come out and face us!"

No one came forward. Nothing moved except that which lived in the forest. Tears of frustration and embarrassment stung my eyes. "I felt it," I said, blinking furiously, telling myself over and over that I wasn't crazy even if, deep down, that fear nearly immobilized me. “Someone was there.”

Bash gathered me into his arms again and pressed a kiss to my temple while he stared into the forest and murmured, “I believe you.”

CHAPTER 6

I eyed the tall, darkly tanned woman standing across the room from me with curiosity seeping from my slightly narrowed eyes as she held her own silent appraisal of me.

Headmistress Donahue, who stood between us, stepped back and raised her hands in a gesture of giving up. "Okay then," she said with a sigh. "How about I leave the two of you to get acquainted." As she walked away, I heard her add, "since neither of you seem to remember your manners," under her breath.

When the door to the room snicked shut, I arched an eyebrow and said in as deadpan a voice as I could manage, "I think we may have fallen short of her highness' formal expectations."

Dalia's stoic expression twitched, then broke, and she slapped a hand over her mouth just a split second too late to hold back the snort of laughter. Her dark eyes lit with amusement as she studied me. "Katherine said I'd like you." She stepped forward with a hand outstretched.

I slipped my hand into hers and shook firmly, keeping my gaze steady and strong. "She told me you were a ball-buster," I said, cocking an eyebrow at the only other natural born Alpha I knew of. "Hopefully she was right on both accounts. I could use another ball-buster in my life."

Dalia sat at one end of the couch, tucking a leg beneath her to face me. "Seems like you're one yourself, so I'm not sure what I could possibly teach you in that area."

All the bravado I'd been storing up abandoned me and I swallowed, trying to push back the barrage of savage emotions that leaped into my throat. I glanced away and up to keep it at bay and managed to stem the tide.

She didn't speak once while I gathered myself, just sat there silently waiting for me to come back. When I looked her in the eye again, there was a knowing there that thoroughly undid the remnants of my control.

I bit down on the inside of my cheek and tasted blood.

"You don't have to do that for me, you know," Dalia said quietly, reaching for a throw pillow to settle on her lap just as I had. She toyed with the edge as she watched me blink furiously. "You don't have to hold yourself together for me."

I sucked my cheeks in and looked up at the chandelier until the tears in my eyes dried again, then met her gaze. "It's not for you," I said in a shaky voice. "If I start now, I won't be able to ask the questions I have and that's more important than blubbering."

Her lips quirked up. "Then why don't we get started. But first," she added, rising to her feet to cross to a small fridge tucked beneath a counter in the corner, "liquid courage. What's your poison?"

I grinned and considered. It wasn't even noon yet, but I was chock full of emotion and finally talking with the only person who could understand part of what I was going through. "Any white wine?" I asked, deciding against anything stronger. I didn't want to get sloppy drunk in front of Dalia Little Foot, natural born Alpha, of all people.

She pulled a bottle of Pinot Grigio from the fridge with a flourish. "Perfect for long discussions about impossible situations." She grabbed two wine glasses and made her way back to the couch.

Once we each had a glass in hand and had taken a long sip, Dalia tilted her head and asked straight out, "What does it feel like to you? The power." She watched me intently.

I considered, wanting to find the right words to describe my experiences. "It was…" I chewed my lip for a moment before meeting her gaze, "seductive." It felt like a lewd confession and brought a blush to my cheeks that burned but Dalia didn't seem to judge me. She just nodded.

"It was like that for me, too, at first," she said with a glimmer of memory. For a second, she was quiet and just looked off as if bringing it all back to mind. Then she blinked and shook her head. "But it didn't stay that way."

I bit my lip again then forced myself to stop. There were too many questions fighting for prominence in my mind that it was hard to pick one to start with. I opened my mouth and just let instinct take over. "What was it like?" I whispered the question. "Sylvie told me a bit about your past. About what the power did to you." I wet my lips with my tongue. "What did it feel like, losing control?" *Did you feel eyes on you when there were none?* I longed to ask, but held it back, for now.

Dalia took a long sip of her drink then stared at the liquid for a moment before answering. "I don't know how much Sylvie told you…"

"Not much," I blurted, realizing it had sounded as if we'd gossiped about the woman. "Just enough to explain why you'd be training me."

"It's alright," Dalia said with a wry smile. "I don't mind. I just think it would be better if I started at the beginning rather than giving you bits and pieces."

I listened as she explained feeling the power rise during each of her pregnancies and then grow along with her children as they grew. I leaned forward at her description of the confidence the power brought, the absolute belief that she was strong enough to handle it, worthy enough to use it only for good.

When Dalia described the surges of anger, of frustration and depression that had begun to plague her, I swallowed hard and listened with rapt attention.

And when she described losing control and lashing out at her innocent children with the power, I squeezed my eyes shut and remembered the way my Alpha voice had boomed from me and taken strong wolves to their knees.

"It started small, you know, the way addictions do," Dalia said in a voice haunted by the past. I could tell it cost her to speak to me, so I stayed quiet and just listened. "And don't fool yourself, it is an addiction, to the power, to that feeling of invulnerability. That's why not everyone tested gets the Alpha ring." She downed the rest of her wine and set the empty glass on the coffee table then returned to picking at the throw pillows edges.

Her eyes were filled with tears when she met my gaze this time. “Elena, I hurt my children. I thought I could control the power until it snapped my mind and turned me into a monster. That’s how my children saw me. As a monster.” A tear spilled down her cheek and fell onto her shirt, unstopped.

Fear gutted me. So much of what she’d described had already happened to me and I was way younger than she’d been. I’d already used the power against others, willingly, and decided to do so because my instincts had said it was the right call. The only call.

But how can I trust my own instincts? Am I being poisoned by this power?

“How did you learn to control it?” It burst out of me, the big question, the one I’d been sitting on, trying to hold back long enough to let her explain her story. It was propelled by an eruption of emotion too powerful to deny any longer. “How do I control it before it controls me?” I whispered.

Dalia’s hand shot out and gripped my forearm tightly. “You won’t have to lose control like I did, Elena. I promise.” Her eyes shined bright with fervent determination. “I won’t let you.” Her chest rose and fell in perfect rhythm with mine.

I stared into her dark eyes for what felt like forever, searching for even a flicker of nerves or trepidation and managed a shaky nod when I found none. She’d been to Hell and back and had survived. No, I argued with myself, she’d learned to thrive, and I could, too.

I just didn't need to take the trip to Hell first. I hoped.

The tension that had descended on the room like a thick fog dissipated as we each sat back and took cleansing breaths. When I caught her gaze again, there was laughter in their depths, the kind I'd become intimately familiar with lately.

"That was intense," I murmured, biting back the scathing snark that tipped my tongue.

Dalia inclined her head in a regal nod and said in a deadpan tone, "Just imagine if we'd broken out the Alpha powers. We could have brought the school body to their knees."

My eyes widened and, for a moment, I wasn't sure if it was a joke or she was serious. I'd felt the lure of my Alpha voice after my first outburst. I couldn't imagine the seductive call Dalia felt every day. I eyed her without saying a word until I saw the quirk of her lips and whooshed out a breath of relief.

"I thought you were serious!" I exclaimed, slapping her lightly on the arm.

Dalia laughed and shook her head. "We'll save the devastation and world dominance for a later session and just focus on control and awareness now, deal?" Her eyebrows rose as she waited for my response with a grin.

I pursed my lips as if considering, then offered her a curt nod. "Control now, take over the world later. I'm on board for that."

She chuckled as she moved to a cozy corner I hadn't noticed. It was decked out like a yoga studio, with a wide carpet on the floor, a lovely water feature tucked into the corner, which she turned on, and privacy screens that shut the rest of the room away. Dalia motioned for me to sit and closed us in.

The screens were just rice paper, I thought, not real protection against the outside world, yet my body responded to their closing as if I'd just been surrounded by an army of the most loyal soldiers. The stress that had been my constant companion for months melted away. My mouth fell open as a sigh slipped free.

Dalia took her place across from me and smiled knowingly. "There's something about it that washes it all away." She motioned to the water feature, which was happily burbling water through faded copper. "I brought it with me when Sylvie asked me to come." She gestured towards the screens. "These, as well. I have an exact replica of this…" Dalia made a soft humming sound in her throat, "retreat, in my home. I wondered if it would have the same effect on you."

A soft hum of approval slipped through my lips as I traced the details of the screens with the tip of my fingers then moved onto the thick carpet beneath me. It felt luxurious, feminine, and powerful. I smiled at Dalia and nodded. "It's working."

"Then let's get started," she said, turning to grab a bag tucked into the corner of our oasis. From it she pulled a deep copper colored bowl and a wooden stick free and placed them between us. "This is a Tibetan singing bowl," Dalia explained. "It's used in meditation and relaxation, both of which will be an extremely important part of your life from now on if it isn't already."

"I've been meditating with Dr. Mira's help," I

explained, eyeing the bowl. I wondered how it would help me focus.

"You hold it like this." Dalia picked up the bowl and balanced it on the tips of her fingers. "Or in the palm of your hand. You don't want to cup it, or the sound will be absorbed by your hand." She picked up the stick with her other hand and gently rubbed it around the outside of the bowl.

The sound started softly, a tremulous pitch that wavered slightly as Dalia rotated the stick around the bowl. It built with each rotation, growing in intensity, reaching a higher, stronger pitch, until it seemed to fill the air around us. It reverberated out, through the floor, through my skin, ignoring anything in its way, until it seemed as if it were a part of me.

I blinked when Dalia handed me the stick and the bowl. I hadn't realized she'd stopped playing. The vibrations still rang through me, pushing out any negative thoughts or self-doubt. I raised my gaze to hers and let out a choked laugh. "That feels really weird."

"Weird or different?"

"Both, I think," I murmured, taking the bowl in my hand. "It feels like I melted away a bit."

She nodded. "That's good. Don't fight it. Just let it take you when your body and mind need to go."

I stared at the bowl for a moment then lifted the stick and began moving it around slowly. It felt a little different this time, I realized, now that it was my hands creating the sound, my hand connected to the bowl. The resonance felt deeper, more elemental as it moved through that small connection and through my entire being. I closed my eyes and let it pull me under.

"Elena." Dalia's voice reached into the stillness and tugged gently, pulling me back from the peace. I resisted for a moment, not wanting the solitude to end, then slipped back to awareness. When I opened my eyes, I found her watching me with a smile. "How was it?"

"Not long enough," I said with a laugh. I could have gone back under in a heartbeat.

Dalia shot me a knowing smile. "You were meditating for over two hours, Elena."

My eyebrows shot up in surprise. "Seriously? Did I keep rubbing the bowl?"

She nodded. "The entire time. Do you remember any of what you experienced in your meditation?"

I frowned, trying to remember anything from the stillness, then shook my head. "No. It was just quiet and peaceful. Was that wrong?"

"No, it's what you needed. When your mind is rested and stronger, you'll experience other things." Dalia pushed to her feet and offered me a hand, which I took without thought.

I stretched and was surprised to find my muscles relaxed after sitting so long on the floor. While Dalia pushed back the screens, I thought about how wonderful I felt, inside and out. It was like a weight had been lifted from me for that short time. It felt amazing, it felt freeing, and it made me realize just how much I'd been carrying these last few months.

"Do you think I'll be alright?" I asked, slipping the bowl and stick back into the bag and placing it in the corner. Now that the weight had been momentarily lifted, I needed to know there was hope it would stay away for good.

Dalia considered me for a long moment, which I found reassuring. She wouldn't give me the answer I wanted, she'd give me the truth. "I think so. We caught it early." Dalia shut off the trickling water feature and turned with a reassuring smile that reflected in her deep brown eyes. "It's not like you've been hearing the voices or anything." She said it as a statement, not a question, as she strode across the room and grabbed a bottle of water from the mini fridge. "Want one?" she asked, grabbing two before I could answer and tossing one to me.

I caught it easily and untwisted the cap automatically, my fingers gripping the plastic so tightly it spun off without barely a thought. I raised the bottle to my lips and drank long and deep, as my heart pounded painfully in my chest and the voices that had begun to tickle the edges of my mind whispered like the dregs of a nightmare.

CHAPTER 7

I took a sip of my coffee and tried not to wince at the overly saccharin taste of it. Daniella had been thoughtful enough to order me a drink, so it was the least I could do to drink it. I tried not to shift in my seat, even though the childish part of me wanted nothing more than to fidget under the expectations of this "casual" chat.

"So," I said, setting the cup down on the table before me. "What were you thinking for the party?"

I focused on the party, not knowing what else to possibly talk to Daniella about, since we hadn't exactly been besties in the months since I'd started at Alpha Wolf Academy. I tried not to let my eyes harden or hands clench as I remembered just how much of a bitch she'd been to me in those first few weeks. We'd made strides since then to come to terms and most often tolerated each other just fine. Then, after the plane crash, something had shifted between us and I'd thought things would be better. Based on the unease coursing through my body, I wasn't so sure I was right.

Based on the way Daniella kept shifting her gaze from me to over my shoulder, I didn't think she was comfortable either. I bit down on the inside of my cheek to stop myself from glancing back, even though the shivers of awareness still skidded over my skin. We were in the dining room, surrounded by students. There were no assassins here. Viktor wasn't here. I swallowed the tremor of fear and concentrated on planning my mate's twenty-third birthday party.

"I was planning on having it at Whistler," Daniella said, setting her cup down. "But I think it'll be better to have it closer to campus." She drummed her perfectly polished nails against her wine stained lips and smiled. "Bash isn't big on going anywhere at the moment."

Because of me, I thought, guiltily. I didn't say it out loud, though, didn't even give it time to sink into my thoughts before I shoved the guilt away. I was working on rejecting negative emotions and thoughts and, so far, it was helping. Besides, I realized, watching Daniella's gaze flit away again, the change in venue wasn't just for Bash or me. Daniella didn't want to leave. She just had a convenient excuse not to take the responsibility for that decision and was using it. I decided to let it be and simply nodded.

"Any ideas where? You know campus a lot better than I do." She'd had a full year of school here before I'd showed up and disrupted her life by falling in love with her twin.

Daniella pursed her lips and tapped them as she mulled it over. "We could just use one of the student lounges or the clearing out in the woods."

The pinched look on her face told me clearly enough

that she didn't like either of those options and I knew that the night would be more special for Bash if his sister was happy. So, I considered what I knew of campus from when I'd searched the maps for the location of The Sisterhood's meeting hall. I leaned in and kept my voice low.

"Katherine told me that when she was here, they used to throw secret parties right on campus under the administration's noses. It wasn't in that location." I raised my eyebrows to covertly reference the huge room under the education building. "So, there has to be another place. Maybe if I ask her..."

Daniella's emerald eyes shone. "We could throw a secret party right here on campus!" She grinned. "Maybe a themed party, like the roaring twenties. It could be like prohibition!"

She sounded so excited at the prospect, I couldn't help but grin back. "If there is something here, I'll find out. Tonight. I'm supposed to have a video chat with her and Quinn anyway."

Daniella's eyes narrowed slightly, and she leaned forward. "What's that like? Being all friendly with the Alpha family after growing up in the country?"

I didn't take it as an insult. I could have, I supposed, and I certainly would have just a few months ago, but I'd experienced enough of Daniella's straight forward way of speaking that I understood she meant no harm with the question.

I considered my response and took another sip of the sweet coffee to give myself time. "It's weird," I said, settling on the truth. "The most important person I ever spoke to before coming here was the town mayor and she's not exactly big shit."

She smiled awkwardly, probably because she didn't know what to say to my small-town experience. I *was* small-town and proud of it, most of the time. Other times it was too overwhelming for pride.

We each sipped at our drinks and glanced away. I fought for something to say, something to add to the conversation about the party but, really, there was nothing that could be done until I talked with Katherine. The silence built until it became a tangible thing between us, a wall of discomfort that I couldn't figure out how to scale.

I was considering making my excuses and leaving when the click, click, click of heels on the wooden floor alerted me to the approach of the bitch squad. Loosing an audible sigh, I turned my head to see Seraphina leading her group of cronies towards our table.

"Your minions are here," I mumbled to Daniella, whose eyebrow simply arched up at the dig.

"Daniella," Seraphina said in the fake nice tone reserved for the very best of bitches. "We were looking for you everywhere. What on earth are you doing *here*?" She looked me directly in the eye and sneered for a split second, then her perfect toothy smile returned.

Daniella took her time answering. She kept her gaze level with Seraphina's as she finished the last sip of coffee and put the cup down on the table. "I was in the mood for coffee," she explained simply, keeping her smile cool and polite. "Why were you looking for me?"

Seraphina's laugh rang out and echoed off the walls of

the dining hall. "Why, to start planning for your birthday party, of course! You didn't think we'd forget, did you? I mean, you have been a bit withdrawn lately, but that's understandable given what you've been through, poor dear."

I felt Daniella's hackles rise. If she'd been withdrawn from the group, it was probably because they thought it was a good idea to call her a "poor dear." Daniella was nobody's "poor dear."

"I've actually just been planning the party with Elena," Daniella said with a flash of teeth.

"Ohhh," Seraphina drew out the word and looked back and forth between us with surprise darkening her blue eyes. Calculation replaced the surprise a moment later as she regarded us. "I see." She fluttered her pretty eyelashes, obviously extensions, and motioned to the chair I was already sitting in. "Well then, I should join you. Elena." Seraphina arched a haughty eyebrow. "You don't mind grabbing another chair, do you?" It was said with a glaze of sweetness that came off faker than her fucking eyelashes.

My heart raced wildly, thundering so loud it almost drowned out the sound of her annoying perky voice. I dug my nails into my palms under the table and forced oxygen into my lungs as I tried desperately to recall the sound of the singing bowl and the peace it had offered.

My awareness sharpened to a pinpoint, focused solely on keeping the part of me that was still wild under control. My emotions were a funnel for it, Dalia had explained. The angrier I was, the sadder, the happier, it was all a possible trigger.

So, I focused on my breath and the floor beneath my feet, and the twinge of pain from my nails cutting into my palms that centered me, and my awareness began to return.

What I returned to was a scene straight out of Mean Girls.

Daniella was on her feet, shoulders drawn back and eyes glinting as she stared down Seraphina. Her wine stained lips might as well have been stained in blood with the icy dressing down she was delivering to the person who had once been her best girl friend on campus while the rest of the voiceless peons stood shaking behind the blood red Seraphina.

"Perhaps next time, you should remember your place, Seraphina, or," Daniella offered a smile that dripped with vitriol, "remember mine." Her gaze darted to me and I saw a moment of fury in her eyes along with asked permission to out my real status on campus, in North American, and in the world.

I shook my head with the slightest movement, so little that anyone else would have missed the gesture, but Daniella understood. She turned her laser gaze back to Seraphina and took a step forward, forcing the flustered girl back. "My life, my actions, my choices, are none of your business, do you hear me?" She said each word separately like punches to the gut.

Seraphina sputtered, losing actual spit as she stammered out words of shock and outrage to which Daniella just raised a hand and responded, "Now, fuck off, Seraphina," and turned away.

"Let's go find Bash, shall we?" She smiled brightly down at me and held out a hand.

I stared at it for a split second before sliding my palm into hers. She gave a tug that brought me to my feet with a laugh that bubbled up, surprising me with its lightness. I searched for the darkness that had been creeping up a moment before and found it all but gone. Gratitude swamped me.

We strode away with heads high and shoulders back, her being the epitome of class, me pretending to be Sylvie LaFlamme. When we stepped through the wide doors of the dining hall and rounded the corner, disappearing from the bitch squads stunned sight, we doubled over in laughter and raced away, side by side, thick as thieves.

My heart leaped with joy as we ran, darting around students and older faculty who shot us disapproving glances that just made us laugh harder. I watched her out of the corner of my eye, dark hair billowing behind as she grinned like a child who just happened to be running on Louboutins. I'd never seen her look so free or so happy, not even when she was with Bash.

We stopped when we made it down the steps of the building and turned towards a little alcove outside with benches and flowers. Thankfully, not the blackberry patch, I thought with a wild giggle.

I collapsed on a bench and shook my head, not quite believing the scene we'd just made, Daniella and I, two opposite sides of a feud that had started the moment we'd laid eyes on each other.

"That was epic!" I said, locking away the memory of seeing the look of utter shock on Seraphina and her bitch squad's faces when Daniella had verbally smacked them down publicly. "But I thought they were your friends?"

Daniella threw her head back and laughed. "Those bitches aren't anyone's friends. They're just minions without a single coherent thought between them." Her shoulders slumped. "They were useful and convenient, but they have never been my real friends." She made air quotes around "friends."

The smile slipped from my lips. "Then, who do you have?" I thought of Sara and Bethany and now Rory. I didn't know how I'd manage to stay sane without them.

Daniella blinked slowly, as if only just realizing something. She frowned, chewed her lip, then raised her eyebrows in surprise. "I don't have any friends."

"Of course, you do," I said automatically, picturing the hordes of people who fawned over Daniella all the time.

"No," she replied, drawing out the word. "I don't. Not really. I have Bash and he's always been enough. Other than him, I have minions." She quirked her lips to the side and shrugged.

Sadness for her, for the loneliness she must feel struck me hard, followed immediately by a dawning of realization for why she'd hated me at first sight. Bash was her world and I was a door crasher. I blew out a breath, considered holding back as I'd been for months now, then went with instinct and spoke from the heart.

"I love your brother more than I thought it was possible and he loves you." Daniella looked up with eyes that sparkled with emotion. I licked my lips and forged on. "Which means you and I have no choice in this world but to love each other, too."

Her lips quirked up as she studied me, saying nothing for a moment that seemed to drag out. Butterflies of nerves danced in my stomach. It was nerve wracking to expose your throat to a predator.

Daniella nodded slowly, still eyeing me. "I hated you from the moment I saw you in Bash's arms, you know."

The butterflies died a painful death then sunk like stones in my belly.

But she wasn't finished. "It was the spark in his eyes that did it." She looked off as if remembering it. "I'd never seen him look at anyone like that before. Not even me." Her voice dipped low.

She was jealous, I realized with a start. I opened my mouth to comment but snapped it shut when she echoed my thoughts.

"We've always had this connection between us. Many twins do, I guess. But it doesn't matter if others have it, too, what we have is…" she shook her head and smiled, "so special I can't even put words to it. I don't think I could survive without him." Daniella pushed up from the bench and began to pace. She fidgeted with the emerald ring she wore, the feminine version of one Bash wore as well. Her eyes were damp when she looked up at me again. "He might be your soul mate, but…"

"He's the other part of your soul," I said quietly, finishing her thought. "I know." I stood up and reached for her, to stop her pacing and calm her fears. "I've always known, which is part of the reason why it was so hard to know you hated my guts so much."

She winced.

"But knowing and feeling are two different things," I

continued, seeing the regret on her face. "And after the crash…" I breathed out a sigh. "You were there, you felt it." I hoped, anyway. She'd felt something, I knew that, but I wasn't sure if it was the same thing I'd experienced.

"Yeah," she confirmed, settling something nervous inside me, "I felt it, too." She chewed her lip. "I've never heard of a connection like that outside of a mate bond before."

I shrugged. "Neither have I, but, honestly, before I met Bash, I wasn't exactly sure soul mates were real."

"Seriously? You've never met any soul mates?" She looked disbelieving.

"I have," I said contemplatively, remembering Sara's and Bethany's parents, whose love was unquestionable. "But my parents aren't, so I guess I was just a bit jaded."

Daniella sat on the edge of the bench. "My parents are soul mates, but my grandparents aren't, so I know what you mean. Did your parents know who you really are?" she asked in a whisper then looked around to make sure no one was close by.

I took a deep breath and sat next to her. "Yes, they knew my entire life."

"And they didn't tell you?" Daniella said in a quiet voice edged with annoyance. It felt good, I realized, hearing her indignant on my behalf. She was the other half of my mate's soul. Part of me craved her approval. "Assholes," she mumbled beneath her breath.

"No," I defended them automatically, feeling the clutch in my stomach at the insult. "They're amazing and they love me like their own. I never felt anything less than loved."

She didn't say anything, just looked out at the people wandering by and waited for privacy again. The silence grew between us again, giving awkwardness time to settle in.

I scanned the students who swarmed by and realized with a start that class must have just let out to have so many people roaming. "Shit," I grumbled, pulling out my phone to see the time. "I'm going to be late for class if I don't beat it." I took a step towards the path and stopped, then turned and inclined my head. "You coming?" I asked, as if it were the most natural thing in the world to do even though it felt weird coming out of my mouth.

Daniella paused for a beat then nodded and fell into step beside me, chasing the awkwardness away. Our relationship wasn't perfect, I was well aware of that fact, but it was a hell of a lot better than it had been back in September.

We stepped out onto the stone path being criss crossed by students and faculty alike and matched our pace to the flow. I considered asking her to meet for another coffee tomorrow but remembered I was meeting with Xavier about the book and fell silent again.

I was just opening my mouth to ask if she'd be up for joining Bash and I for a movie when Daniella's hand shot out and grabbed me by the arm. She jerked me so hard I stumbled and went flying with her behind a bush on the corner of the science building.

My heartbeat exploded painfully, thundering against my ribs as every survival instinct I had went on overdrive. I scanned the crowd with eyes wide with fear. "What? Where?" I asked, breathy and terrified.

Daniella's fingers tightened on my arm, tugging me around as she pointed at a group of guys standing at the far end of the building, chatting and laughing. "There," she hissed, pointing at them. "The one with the long black hair."

I stared at him, at them, then rotated my head to stare at her. "Old Ones, Daniella!" I scolded, yanked my arm away from her claws. "You scared the shit out of me. I thought we were under attack again."

Her face drained of color then bloomed a bright red that almost matched her lipstick. Baffled, I leaned out from behind our hiding spot and sized up the guy that was apparently making her crazy. He was tall, well over six feet, and wide in the shoulders. His dark hair was loose around a face the color of bronze.

"Ohhh," I said, grinning. "He's gorgeous. Who is he? I haven't seen him around campus before." Curiosity chased away the terror and calmed my racing heart.

"His name is Grayson," she whispered, peeking out again. "Grayson LittleFoot."

I blinked in surprise, recognizing the name right away. "As in..."

"As in the youngest son of Jacob LittleFoot, Sylvie's co-Alpha," Daniella said on a slow exhalation. "And," she added, tearing her gaze from him to meet mine, "I think, my soul mate."

CHAPTER 8

"Your supporting characters are falling a little flat," Xavier said with a frown, tapping the manuscript in front of him. "You're going to need to go back and flesh out your character descriptions."

I nodded and scribbled a note in the journal I kept specifically for this project. I'd been meeting with Xavier once a week since the plane crash to discuss my current work in progress, a big fat pile of crap as far as I was concerned, but a promising idea according to him.

Besides Bash and Rory, writing was my solace. It got me out of my head and gave me distance from the fears that constantly swirled in my brain and put me squarely in another world. The fact that my world with its dystopian society lead by a despot leader who was very closely modeled after my insane uncle, might not have been the healthiest thing in the world, but it was helping me cope. I'd heard it said before that authors have amazing coping skills. If we were hurt, damaged, happy, sad, whatever… it didn't matter, we just wrote about it. We purged the feelings from our hearts and souls and minds onto the page and felt better for it.

I wondered when I'd feel completely better. I assumed it wouldn't happen anytime soon, not unless someone managed to take out Viktor and free me from the impending doom of his death threats.

Fuck, my life was complicated.

"Think about your favorite TV shows," Xavier said, pushing up from his desk chair to wander to the mini fridge set in the corner. He lifted a bottle of water with a raised eyebrow and brought it to me when I nodded and murmured "thank you."

I considered what he was saying and thought of my favorite show, Buffy the Vampire Slayer. Buffy was a great character, there is no doubt in that, but it was the Scooby gang that really made the show complete. The development of Willow, Xander, and even Giles pushed the plot forward, kept it interesting. I scratched another note in my journal. "Okay, I see what you mean. I've developed Clarissa and her mother, but Donovan and Sadie need more back story and motivation."

He twisted the top off his bottle of water and took a long drink, then nodded. "Exactly, like my favorite book series, Game of Thrones. Those books would be nothing if each supporting character wasn't fully developed, and there are a million different characters. The coolest part about that series, I find, is that the characters you think are supporting might actually turn out to be more important than you first thought. What's your favorite show?"

"Buffy," I said without hesitation. I shot him a grin.

"Kick ass girl, pretty hair, sexy guy, what more could you ask for?"

He chuckled. "No, I get it. Buffy is the perfect example of what I mean. Characters like Willow, who started in a supporting position, eventually became just as important to the plot, if not more, than Buffy herself."

"Okay." I nodded, knowing he was right. "What did you think about the hook at the end of chapter seven?" I chewed my lip while waiting for him to respond and hoped he liked it. I was particularly proud of the punch to the jugular I'd delivered there.

His lips perked up. "I'm not going to lie," he started, making my heart sink. "I might have cursed you when I read it. I didn't see it coming, at all, and it kinda blew my mind." He chuckled. "Elena, this book is going to be amazing. You've got a talented and warped mind, two things absolutely necessary for creativity."

The breath I'd been holding whooshed out of me and the tension in my stomach dissipated. "You really liked it?" I heard the nerves and uncertainty in my voice and wished I didn't feel it so intensely. It was embarrassing.

Xavier's eyebrow arched up. "You think that I'd hold back if I didn't?"

I laughed, remembering the display of red ink splayed across the first essay I completed for his class. It had been a bloodbath and had devastated me, especially since, at the time, I'd been under the assumption that my presence at Alpha Wolf Academy was partially due to his recommendation based on my writing. He'd been a bit of a jackass those first few weeks, mostly because his personal life had been falling apart, and I'd thought the mentor/mentee relationship I'd been looking forward to with him was an impossibility. Then I'd saved his life after the attack on campus and he'd come around. Now, these weekly meetings were at the top of my list of priorities, right there with The Sisterhood, my training, my soulmate, and my friends.

"Alright," he said, moving back behind his desk. "Instead of working on chapter eight this week, why don't you add to those character descriptions in your book Bible. Then rework the sections where Donovan and Sadie appear. You've done a really good job of describing the setting and creating the mood, so adding to their characters should level up what you've done so far. Plus," he added with a nod towards my manuscript, "that hook will be even more effective if the reader cares more about the supporting characters."

I chewed my lip as I wrote a few more notes then snapped my journal shut and looked up with a grin. "Got it. And, if I haven't said it already a million times, thank you for this."

Xavier lifted his hands like a martyr and said in a deadpan tone, "I live to serve." He laughed when I smacked him on the arm with my journal.

I gathered up my stuff, folding the manuscript he'd scribbled notes on into my journal, and stood to leave. I had a biology class starting in less than an hour that I needed to get ready for.

"Hey," Xavier called out as I opened the door to his office. "I know it's traditional for authors and all artists, really, to question their abilities. But you're good, Elena, and you're only going to get better with time and experience."

I hugged his words tight to my chest and nodded because my throat was too filled with emotion to speak. By the look in his eyes, which were filled with pride, I knew he understood what that kind of praise meant to me. I slipped through the open door and closed it with a click then rushed back to my room with a smile plastered across my face, and joy in my heart.

♀ ♀ ♀

I stretched my neck and groaned at the satisfying snap of spine. I'd been working on my character sketches between classes and sexy times with Bash for the last couple of days and was fairly confident that I'd given Donovan and Sadie real personalities and quirks that would give them room to grow and develop.

I was stiff, bored, and ready for some fun. But Bash was busy playing rugby on the far side of campus for the rest of the evening, so sexy times were out of the question, at least until after his game, when he came home sweaty, and dirty, and...

"Whoa," I said on a laugh, pushing to my feet. I was pretty hard-up when the thought of my soulmate, dirty and sweaty, made my thighs tighten. It wasn't as if I was actually hard up, in fact, I had more sex in the last couple of weeks than I ever had in my life. There is just something *more* about being with the other part of your soul that made physical contact or emotional contact, for that matter, tantalizing.

I wasn't the philosophical type, not really, but I'd given a bit of time to thinking about the bond between soulmates. It wasn't perfect. It wasn't supposed to be perfect. He still annoyed the shit out of me sometimes as, I'm sure, I did him. But even when I was annoyed with him, I wanted to be with him, to touch him, to taste him. And when we weren't together, physically in the same space, I still felt him. He was as much a part of me now as the blood that ran in my veins. Our new connection only added to that intimacy.

We tested it out, the limits to our new bond. It turned out, that we could communicate psychically from the far corners of campus. We hadn't gone beyond those borders, due to the fact that a psychopath was trying to murder me, but we both assumed there was no limit. That was comforting, and sexy as hell.

Of course, he didn't hear my every thought and I didn't hear his. To send our thoughts, we had to project them, focus on sending them. With an evil grin, I bit down on my lower lip and sent him a particularly vivid image of what I would like to do to him tonight after his game.

I felt his response immediately and dissolved into laughter when I felt him fall flat on his face in the muddy field.

Sorry, I thought at him, trying to hide my amusement.

Old Ones, woman! he sent back with obvious exasperation. This wasn't the first time I'd sent him mental porn, nor would it be the last, I thought. *You nearly killed me*! I thought for a moment that he'd just go back to the game, but a second later, he sent back a thundering wave of love and desire so huge that it floored me.

I staggered to my bed and sat as my legs turned to jelly.

I'll see you tonight, Bash thought with another flash of lust, then disappeared.

"Wow. That escalated quickly," I murmured fanning myself with my hand. When my legs were steady enough to hold me up, I made my way to the bathroom and took a quick shower. My body was buzzing with energy and I needed an outlet that wasn't sexual, so I grabbed my phone and texted Rory.

Girl's night?

I could fit in time with the girls before jumping my mate. I didn't have to wait long for her response.

What do you have in mind?

Rory and I hadn't had the chance to hang out since the party, so I figured I may have snacks, movies, and chatting would do us both good.

Pajamas, pizza, wine, and Dirty Dancing. You can bring Addison if you want.

I knew what it was like, discovering your soulmate and wanting to spend every moment with them. Bash and I had been together for almost six months now, but my desire to be with him had only increased in that time. Besides, I really wanted to get to know my best friend's soulmate a bit better, even if seeing her made me feel guilty for Adeline's death.

Sounds fun. She says she'd love to. What time?

I glanced at the time, surprised that it was so late in

the evening. The day had completely gotten away from me.

8:00 PM good?

Perfect. We'll bring the pizza.

I've got the wine. See you then.

Byeeeeee.

I grinned at her farewell and pulled off my towel, letting it drop on the floor at my feet. For a real girl's night, there was only one choice in attire. I pulled a cheetah print onesie from my pajama drawer and pulled it on over my underwear. A pair of thick wool socks, hand knitted by my Nan, completed the ensemble. I quickly braided my hair, which had sprouted another three inches since Christmas, and grinned at my reflection. I was ready.

My phone dinged a moment later and I picked it up, expecting another text message from Rory. Instead, I saw one from Daniella.

Hey, want to do something tonight? Bash is busy with his guy friends, so I know you two aren't canoodling. ;-)

My smile faded. I didn't want to lie to her, but I also didn't think Rory would feel comfortable having Daniella join us for girl's night. She and I had just started to understand one another, I couldn't really expect someone else, someone who had been the butt of more than one of Daniella's jokes over the years, to feel the same way. Still, it felt wrong to leave her out. Especially after Daniella had confessed to having no girlfriends, or real friends, for that matter, on campus or off. I switched over to my chat with Rory and typed out the question.

Okay, I know you're going to hate this idea, but what would you think of Daniella joining us tonight?

I waited three seconds and winced when I saw her response.

Are you insane?!

I sighed and tried to explain.

I know. She's a bitch. And she's been a bitch to you many times. But I'm connected to her through Bash and, I don't know, we talked, and things are better. She's Bash's twin, Rory.

I felt Rory's reluctance in the time it took for her to write a response and was flooded with guilt from both sides as she typed.

Fine. But you better have lots of wine.

I smiled.

I have six bottles and Doritos.

I make no promises, okay?

I chewed my lips and tried to imagine the possible ways tonight could end. Screaming, punching, World War III. I sighed and wrote back.

Deal.

I hit send then put down my phone and assessed my room. It was pretty clean but could use some work. I set to work, gathered my supplies, and prepared for war.

CHAPTER 9

Rory stared at Daniella. Daniella stared at Rory. Addison shifted nervously and took another sip from her glass. I rolled my eyes so hard I saw the back of my brain and sighed.

"So," I started, feeling the need to break the building tension with words. "What movie do you guys want to watch? I have Dirty Dancing, The Greatest Showman, Bridesmaids, and Mean Girls."

"Mean girls," Rory said in a decisive tone, leveling her gaze on Daniella who just arched an eyebrow and didn't say a word.

"Oh, I love Dirty Dancing so much," Addison said with a hesitant smile. "It's my mom's favorite movie. She watches it every time it comes on TV. Plus, she owns it on DVD, Blu-ray, and even VHS. Not that anyone has VHS players anymore, but she won't get rid of it."

I licked my lips and offered Addison a smile. She and I were the only ones in the room who weren't acting like giant jackasses, so we'd be in charge of choosing the movie. "Dirty Dancing it is, then." Since it was on Netflix, I turned on the streaming service and typed in the title.

I popped the cork on the second bottle of Pinot Grigio and topped up mine and Addison's glasses then, without asking, topped up Rory's and Daniella's as well. I wasn't sure if adding alcohol to the mix would make things better or worse, but something had to happen, and soon, or they were going to drive me crazy.

We settled in, three of us on my bed and Daniella in the chair next to the window. I'd forgotten to fill Daniella in on the expected dress code, so she was the only one wearing jeans. She hadn't said a lot since arriving with two bags full of candy, chips, and chocolate. And not just any chocolate, I'd realized with intense pleasure as she'd emptied out the bags on my desk. Daniella Reeves didn't show up to a party, even as something as simple as a girl's night, with Kit Kat bars or even the Christmas favorite, a box of Pot of Gold. No, she brought an assortment of Godiva, Marie Belle, and Jacques Torres chocolates, plus a box of perfectly made macarons in pale pinks, blues, and greens. Even Rory hadn't been able to turn up her nose at the offerings.

By the time we got to the big dancing at the Sheraton Hotel, we made our way through three bottles of wine and a good chunk of the food. I groaned and rubbed my tummy, then reached for the remote and pause the movie.

"I have to pee so bad," I said with a moan as I pushed myself up off the bed.

"Me too," three other voices echoed.

Being a good hostess, I let the others go first, reassuring them that I was okay for the moment when I was on the verge of peeing in my leopard print onesie. When Daniella came out, I raced in and slammed the door.

When I emerged a few minutes later Rory and Addison were helping themselves to another slice of pizza while Daniella was filling her glass from another bottle she'd opened. She took the bottle towards my glass. "Want a refill?"

"Sure," I said crossing the room to lift my glass. I was already well on my way to being sloshed, but that was the best part about a girl's night, if you got too drunk all you had to do was fall asleep. Or dance it off.

I grabbed the remote again and turned the movie back on, then began to shake my ass as the music began to play. I put my glass down and reached out a hand to Rory who, without a second's hesitation, slipped her hand into mine and moved into a perfect twirl. Addison laughed and clapped, and even Daniella broke a grin.

We re-created the scene, then moved on to other scenes and, 10 minutes later, were rolling on the floor laughing after several failed attempts at the final lift, one of which had Addison tossed neatly onto the bed after I couldn't hold her up for more than two seconds.

"I can do this," I said, climbing to my feet again. "I'm strong, see?" I flexed my muscles to show them my defined biceps. They made satisfactorily impressive sounds at my display. Even I was impressed by how much progress I'd made lately. "Who's going to be my Baby?"

Rory shook her head. "I can't! I might pee myself."

"I'm out, too," Addison said with a giggle. "I think I hurt myself that last time." She stretched her neck to the side and winced.

I eyed Daniella, whose eyes went wide as she turned and tried to run into the bathroom, shouting, "No! Not me."

I plopped down into my chair and pouted my lip. "You guys are mean. You don't trust me."

Daniella peeked out from the bathroom. "I trust you with my brother. That counts, right?"

I brightened. "That *does* count," I said, nodding towards her. "He's the best. Like, literally the best. I have no idea what I did to deserve him." I shook my head in wonder.

"No," Rory said, crossing the room to climb to my lap. "You're the best. He's a lucky one to deserve you." She nodded emphatically as if wiser words had never been spoken. Addison agreed by bobbing her head up and down.

"You guys are all lucky," Daniella said, stepping out from the bathroom. She climbed onto the bed and sat, crossed legged, never once tipping her glass. "I want a boyfriend. I want Grayson." She pouted and drained the rest of her glass, which had just been filled, then looked confused as to where her wine had gone.

"Who's Grayson?" Addison asked reaching for the bag of Doritos.

"Grayson is our newest transfer student. He's tall, dark, gorgeous, and just happens to be the son of Jacob LittleFoot, and Daniella's new crush." I fluttered my eyelashes at her and grinned when she laughed like a normal girlfriend, rather than my arch nemesis.

Rory frowned. "Why is he just getting here now? It's awfully late in the year to start a new school, isn't it?"

Daniella shrugged. "I'm not sure," she murmured, blushing a delicate shade of rose that made her look only more beautiful.

I goggled at her. "Are you saying that you haven't even talked to him yet?" As her cheeks exploded with color at my question, I figured I'd hit the nail on the head. "Are you serious? You, Queen bitch of Alpha Wolf Academy, are intimidated by a male?"

"I knew you called me Queen bitch!" Daniella said with an eye roll. "Bash said I was just being sensitive." She held up two fingers on each side of her head and made quotation marks. "And I am not intimidated by him," she added, lifting her chin high enough to be an actual Queen. "I just don't really know what to say to him." She shrugged and lifted her empty glass to her lips then frowned. "Who drank all my wine?"

I STARTED TO LAUGH. It bubbled out of me in trills that were contagious and soon we were all doubled over and roaring. When we managed to come out of it, Daniella turned to look at Rory, who seemed to have come around to her presence over the course of their drinking, and asked, "Speaking of men. How are you and Darius doing? I see the way you guys are with each other. Can't keep your hands to yourselves." She wagged her eyebrows at Rory, whose face had gone suddenly and completely white.

The tension that had left the room, spiked again in an instant, bringing a look of wariness to Daniella's emerald eyes. She glanced around the room, looking between me and Rory, a frown marring her beauty. "What? What did I say?" She sounded completely confused and I didn't blame her.

Addison's hand moved slowly, almost imperceptibly, and settled on the small of Rory's back, in a simple gesture of reassurance. Daniella's gaze, sharp despite the alcohol in her system, caught the movement and her eyes went wide.

"Holy shit!" She exclaimed, covering her mouth with her hand in shock.

Rory's back went stiff as a board and her face flushed deep crimson. Before I could interject and calm the situation down, she leaped to her feet and shoved her finger in Daniella's face. "What? Are you fucking homophobic, as well as a bitch?" Her chin jutted out in fury in her hands balled into fists.

I jumped up and moved to Rory's side. There was enough alcohol between them to bring down a team of humans, so rational minds were not present.

Daniella surged to her feet and peeked around my shoulder. "I'm not homophobic!" She said in an offended tone. "I was just surprised, that's all. The last time I saw you, you and Darius were an item."

The rage drained out of Rory's face and body, leaving her wilted where she stood. She backed up a few steps and sat on the edge of the bed, then looked down and muttered, "Sorry. But, in my defense, you're usually a huge bitch." The flush of anger was replaced now by embarrassment at having overreacted.

Daniella looked as if she was going to argue back, then just shrugged and accepted the retort. "That's fair. I have been a huge bitch to you." She looked at me and added, "and you. I don't really know you," she said to Addison. "But I'm sure that I would have been a bitch if given time."

Addison nodded and patted her on the shoulder. "We can all be a bit of a bitch sometimes."

I took in the scene before me, encouraged by the lack of blood and hair on my floor. "Okay," I said, with a grin. "That wasn't so bad. I think, to celebrate, we should re-enact the final dance in dirty dancing." I moved to the far end of the room and held my hands up in front of my chest, ready to catch anyone who dared to fly at me.

It worked. The tension dissipated, once more, and was replaced with smiling faces and laughter.

♀♀♀

I must've fallen asleep, because when I opened my eyes, the room was silent. On the TV, Netflix prompted me to let them know if I was still watching. I picked up the remote and clicked it off and looked around the room at the prone bodies lying on the floor and on the bed. The sight of them made me smile as I pushed to my feet.

It was late. The sun had gone down hours ago and the moon, what little sliver there was of it, was high in the night sky, casting its small illumination through my curtains. I stepped around Rory and Addison, who were lying together, snuggled closely on the floor. In repose, Rory's face was the picture of innocence in the hand she had casually placed over Addison's hip, the picture of love.

I left the proof of our overindulgence where it lay, crumpled on the floor, or on my desk, and retreated into the bathroom to relieve my aching bladder. My head still swam a little if I moved quickly but, for the most part, I was sobering up. Overactive metabolisms came in handy.

I switched the light off and closed the door to the bathroom with a soft snick then turned and nearly died of a heart attack when I saw Rory standing two feet in front of me. My hand flew to my chest, covering my heart as it raced wildly.

"Old Ones! You scared the shit out of me." I blew out a deep breath and glanced past her. Daniella and Addison still slept soundly.

"Sorry," Rory whispered. "I heard you get up. I need to pee." She rushed past me to the bathroom and disappeared inside.

I yawned again and wondered what time it was. It was way too early to be awake, that was for sure, but it might be too late to go back to sleep, especially after getting a fright like that. My dreams would be filled with lurking danger and familiar electric blue eyes now if I tried to get a few more hours in. Rory knew about my nightmares, but she'd never been around to see me wake up screaming covered in sweat. The last thing I wanted was for Addison and Daniella to see me like that.

So, despite the absurdity of it, I began gathering up the garbage, staying as quiet as wolfly possible, and wondered what I'd do for the next few hours.

When Rory emerged from the bathroom, she stopped in the doorway and watched me for a moment before speaking. "Not tired?"

I shook my head. "No, not really, but I don't want to wake them up."

Rory covered her mouth as she yawned and nodded

towards the bathroom. "Come on then," she said quietly. "Step into my office. We didn't get the chance to chat earlier. What better time than the middle of the night?"

I grinned and followed her into her office, closing the door behind me.

I loved my bathroom. Back home in Newfoundland, where houses were small and intimate, no one had private bathrooms unless you were rich or the owners of the house. My parents and I had shared a small bathroom my entire life, and the only space in the house that was mine had been my bedroom.

I decorated in shades of dove grey and rose gold, and never failed to smile when I stepped inside. I'd never been particularly girly growing up, it just wasn't as interesting as being a tomboy. But there was a part of me, a part I usually kept well hidden, that reveled in the feminine and the soft. Which is why I'd gone wild in Montréal when buying my supplies for school. Bethany and Sara, who knew me better than anyone in the entire world, hadn't been the least surprised by my choices. In fact, they'd helped me pick out some of the prettiest pieces.

Rory sat on the soft velvet bench I kept in front of the vanity while I sat on the edge of the toilet seat and twisted my back to bring out the last of the fatigue left in my body.

"So," I said, chewing on my lip hesitantly. Rory had been so busy with Addison lately, and I'd been busy with Bash and my character sketches, that we hadn't had the chance to talk about the inevitable breakup. Knowing Rory as I did, I knew she and Darius had had the talk, since she and Addison were out now as an official couple. "How did it go? How is he?"

Rory exhaled softly and looked up with a shake of her head. "It was horrible." She blinked several times rapidly. "Elena, he didn't see it coming. Not at all. He..." Rory struggled for words. My heart went out to her, but I said nothing, knowing she just needed time and someone to really listen.

"He was so confused. He just kept saying how sometimes it took time for the soul mate bond to solidify. He said his own parents were together for three years before they knew." She pushed to her feet and began pacing a small room, fidgeting with her fingers. "But, it's not usually like that, right? I mean, my parents are soul mates, and they knew almost right away. There was a connection between them, like a rubber band that finally snapped into place one day and they could feel each other. I love him, Old Ones know, I love him so much, but I know it's not there. We can wait until the end of time and it still won't be there."

"Did you tell him about Addison?" I asked quietly, knowing the dark-haired girl was the center of Rory's universe.

She nodded and covered her mouth with one of her shaking hands. "He just kept saying it'll happen for us, it just takes time, don't give up. I tried to make him understand without ripping his heart to shreds, but finally I just had to tell him." She held up her hands in defeat. "He could never be my soulmate because Addison already is."

I went to her, crossing the bathroom floor and wrapping her in my arms as her body shivered with grief. She found her soul mate, yes, but she'd also broken the heart of a boy she loved dearly, the first boy she ever loved. I pulled back and smoothed the hair from her forehead.

"It's okay to grieve for what you lost with Darius and still be happy with Addison," I murmured, wishing with all my heart I could ease the ache in hers.

She swallowed and nodded, as her eyes filled with tears that spilled onto her cheeks. "Thank you," she said in a hoarse whisper that was filled with emotion. "I needed to hear that."

"Well, that's what best friends are for, right?"

She smiled, a small twitch of her lips, and a little of the grief in her dark eyes faded. I pulled her in once more and squeezed until she patted my arm like a wrestler trying to get a hold and came up gasping for air.

"Come on," Rory said, tugging me towards the door. "Let's go check out that all night snack bar across campus."

I made a considering face for a split second then grinned. "Sounds perfect. Should we leave them a note?"

Rory crossed to the whiteboard that was a staple in each student room and sprawled a quick note in erasable marker.

Couldn't sleep. Gone out for a walk. Text if you wake up.

"There," she said, grabbing her cell and mine from the bedside table. "That'll do it.," She said with a grin that reached her eyes. "Let's go see if they really do make the best burgers on campus or if that's just a rumor spread by stoners." She blew a kiss towards Addison and followed me out the door as I checked my phone for messages from Bash, who I now considered the soul of patience seeing as

I'd left him with expectations I hadn't met. I'd blow his mind tomorrow, I thought with a wicked grin that faltered as I read the only other message sent that evening.

Sisters make the best friends in the world. ~ Marilyn Monroe

Below the quote was a meme of two cute kittens attacking a broom with the caption, "At midnight we ride!"

CHAPTER 10

The underground room where The Sisterhood met in secret beneath the noses of Alpha Wolf Academy males was buzzing when we descended the hidden stairs and joined our sisters.

"We just had a meeting a month ago," Rory said, leaning in to whisper conspiratorially. "I wonder why they called another one so soon." She tugged at the hem of her dress.

I shrugged and scanned the mass of women, looking for Katherine or Sylvie. Neither had given any indication they'd be on campus tonight, so I was as clueless as everyone else. I didn't like it. To distract myself, I smacked her hand away from her hemline and turned to ask her, "Why are you acting like a virgin on her wedding night? You haven't been able to stop fidgeting since we left your room."

Her hands stilled and she forcibly moved them to her side, then to her hips, then interlaced them in front of her abdomen. "Addison isn't here," she murmured, glancing around as if spies were listening. "I hinted at the meeting tonight, hoping she'd get my meaning and tell me that she's a sister, too, but she said she didn't have plans, and she's not here." Rory chewed on her lip. "I don't think she's a member, yet. So…" she said inhaling deeply, "I was thinking about talking to Katherine about it. If you don't mind, that is." Her hand touched my forearm and her dark button eyes, so sincere and nervous, met mine.

"Of course, I don't mind." I patted her hand and smiled. It had never been my goal in life to run with the big dogs, that was my reality. What was the benefit of having connections if you couldn't use them to help your friends? "Look, they're getting started." I moved towards the front of the room with Rory at my side.

Along the way, Daniella joined us, falling in step as if we'd been a trio forever. I grinned at the thought of the image we projected. The Queen bitch, dressed in emerald green brocade and diamonds, the diminutive sprite, dressed in sapphire silk, and the scholarship kid, dressed in crimson. We hadn't planned it, but together we looked formidable. People actually moved out of our way.

Katherine LaFlamme stepped onto the raised platform at the far end of the room, instantly catching everyone's attention. As the first-born daughter of the country's Alpha, she was a big deal, but not a regular attendee of these meetings. So, when the murmurs of the crowd merely increased with her appearance, I realized she wasn't alone.

Daphne Dru, wife of Keme LittleFoot and daughter-in-law of Dalia, joined Katherine on stage a moment later, followed by another woman with dark golden hair highlighted with auburn. I eyed her, speculating on who she was, and what role she played in The Sisterhood, then gasped and shot my hand out on either side and grabbed my companions.

"That's Rose LaFlamme," I hissed, tugging them closer.

After the fall of the Alpha Council last year, the story of Rose's origin had been revealed to those in the know. I knew nothing of it, not being one of those in the know, until Sylvie and Katherine had filled me in on all the details. My jaw had dropped and stayed open the entire story, which sounded as much like a fairy tale or soap opera as any I've ever known. In a subsequent meeting, Katherine had explained the details to the sisters, as well, so Rory and Daniella knew who she was.

"Seriously?" Rory asked, pressing close to my side. She squinted and whispered, "I can kind of see it."

"I wonder why she's here," Daniella murmured, also pressing close. Apparently, our girl's night had made us thick as thieves in her eyes. "From all reports, she likes to stay pretty far out of the limelight."

I watched them, Katherine and Rose, and the way they moved with each other, as if they'd been sisters their entire lives. I wondered about that, about the friends who became more than friends, became your family and more. It was obvious that more than just their father's blood ran through their veins. They were sisters, true sisters, and seeing them together made my heart swell.

I was blessed. In so many ways, I was blessed, with friends and family, even with Daniella. If it weren't for the small matter of being wanted by a psychopathic murderer, my life would be rainbows and sunshine. I bit back a chuckle.

One last woman climbed the steps to stand with Katherine, Daphne, and Rose in front of the gathering of women. Dalia LittleFoot took her place next to her daughter-in-law, who smiled at her with genuine warmth. Knowing what I did now about Dalia's descent into darkness when her children were young, and the torture she'd put them through, it was good to see that forgiveness was possible. Daphne, of all people, would be protective over her soulmate, Keme, and the hurts inflicted upon him when he was innocent and defenseless.

Taking the lead, Katherine stepped forward and addressed the group "Welcome Sisters. Thank you for coming out on such short notice. I know we met just last month, but we all just happened to be in the area and thought this is a good chance to fill you in on the current efforts of The Sisterhood."

"As you know, the rescue and release of the young women held captive by the rogue wolf, Raphael, last year has been an ongoing effort and labor of love for my sister, Rose." Katherine gestured to the younger woman and prompted her forward.

Rose hesitated for the barest of moments and squared her shoulders and came to stand beside her sister. She raised her voice so that even those at the back of the room could hear.

"A year ago, twenty-nine women were freed from Benbulbin mountain in Ireland. These women are my sisters." She shifted to look at Katherine and corrected her statement. "Our sisters. In the months since, we have collectively looked to the future of wolfdom. We've seen what having an unfit leader, someone whose only goal is power and the degradation of others, can do to a people." Rose sighed and took a deep breath before starting again. "Our world deserves the best leaders it can get, be they male or female, it doesn't matter. The Sisterhood is not here to fight for the female domination of our kind, it is here to fight for the fair representation of our gender in an arena that has been patriarchal for too long."

She stepped closer to the edge of the stage, her eyes lit now with passion and fervor. "Throughout history, women have fought to keep their children safe. That's what we're doing now and will continue to do every day for the rest of our lives. We will help facilitate those who will lead with goodness and fairness as they take their spots in our history books and make our lives better." Her hands fell to her side as she stared out at the crowd with a wide smile that only amplified her beauty.

Katherine clapped along with everyone and moved to wrap her arm around Rose's shoulder. She leaned in to whisper something that made Rose laugh but was too low for anyone else to hear. The sweetness of it, the sheer simplicity of sisters sharing a joke, left emotion thick in my throat.

When the applause died down, Katherine lifted her voice again. "Because we were here anyway, and because we wanted to share excitement of this historic moment with all of you before it hits the news, we decided to deliver it ourselves." She looked over at Daphne and nodded.

Daphne stepped forward, taking Katherine's place, and

addressed the group. "Honestly, I don't know whether to say good evening or a very early good morning. I have no idea why we meet at such auspicious times, but I do like the drama of it all." Laughter tittered through the crowd. "For those who don't know me, I am Daphne LittleFoot, wife to Keme LittleFoot, first-born son of Alpha Jacob LittleFoot. I stand here beside my friends and family to announce with pride and gratitude that as of this evening, two more Alphaships have been granted by the Alpha Council to our sisters."

Surprised silence left her announcement hanging in the air for a split second before hands met with hands and voices raised in excited shouts. I shifted from foot to foot, too overwhelmed by the news to stay still. It was absurd, that in our modern world the news of two women rising to power somewhere in our great wide world would bring so much joy. I'd never followed politics before coming to AWA, of course that was before I learned my place in the world of Alpha politics. I had a good idea which candidates would've passed the Alpha Council's approval and trials. I held my breath and squeezed Rory's and Daniella's hands as Daphne raised her palms in the air to silence the cacophony.

"So, join us in celebrating the new Alphas of Belgium, Elise Heylen, and of Slovenia, Irena Novak!" Daphne threw up her hands and loosed a very unladylike shout that made the group erupt into cheers and laughter.

Servers appeared seemingly out of nowhere with trays of champagne flutes, filled to the brim with golden liquid. I accepted one from a woman I didn't recognize and lifted it into the air in salute to two women I admired greatly. Belgium and Slovenia were in good hands.

The meeting devolved into a party, which no one complained about. After the first round of champagne, glasses of Pinot Grigio and Pinot Noir were passed out like water to thirsty sailors while music pumped out of the speakers I hadn't known were there.

"Best secret society meeting ever!" Rory said on a laugh as she swung her hips side to side and took another drink of wine.

"Now all you need is to have Addison by your side," I said, shimmying my shoulders and watching in awe as Daniella executed a perfect pirouette in her Jimmy Choo's. "Stop showing off," I joked.

"Elena," Katherine's voice had me spinning around, not quite as gracefully as Daniella. Katherine's face was lit up from within and her eyes sparkled. It was nice seeing her so genuinely happy.

I stepped into her open arms and took the hug she always offered. When I stepped back, she gestured towards the woman beside her and made introductions. "Elena, Aurora." Her eyes widened slightly at Daniella's proximity to us in the smile on her usually disgruntled face. "And Daniella," she included, "this is my dear friend Daphne Dru and my sister Rose LaFlamme."

Handshakes and nods were exchanged all around while Katherine shot me a questioning look and glanced towards Daniella. I, in return, gave her the barest of shrugs and lifted an eyebrow, hoping she'd understand that I'd explain later when we weren't in the middle of a party.

"So, what were you guys doing in the area?" I asked, standing with Rory and Daniella opposite three of my personal heroes.

"Keme wanted to visit his mother," Daphne said. "So, we figured why not make a vacation out of it and get the tribe together. With babies and oceans between us, we rarely get the chance to do more than video chat."

"That "oceans between us" dig was directed at me," Rose said, making a face at Daphne who grinned in response. "Liam and I have been pretty busy with the women from Benbulbin. That's partially what brought me back. There are a few academies I want to check out for the girls who want to ease into the world." She held up a hand when Daphne sputtered in mock anger. "And I wanted to see my best friend and sister," she added, mollifying the gorgeous Mi'kmaq woman.

Daphne nodded. "I'll accept it." She snaked an arm around Rose's waist and pulled her in. "Basically, it was an excuse to get together, drink too much wine, reminisce about the times we almost died together, and talk about how sexy our husbands are." She tipped her glass towards us. "You three should join us!"

Katherine laughed and hip bumped her friend. "Daphne is a little drunk," she explained. "She's off mom duty tonight. I'm off mom duty, too!" She did a little hip shake and laughed again. "We've got one of the guest suites over at the far end of campus. Will you guys come party with us old ladies?"

"Speak for yourself, Grandma!" Rose said, taking another sip of her wine. She squealed a moment later and twisted away when Katherine tried to smack her on the leg.

I watched them, unable to tear my gaze away, and couldn't believe where the twists and turns of my life had led.

I was going to a private party with three of the most kickass she wolves on the planet. Life was pretty good.

I smiled brightly, excited about the night ahead, and willed the voices that whispered in my head constantly now to hush.

CHAPTER 11

I slammed my cup down on the table and raised my hands above my head with a raucous cheer immediately echoed by Katherine. A chorus of jeers followed from the two other teams.

"Sore losers!" Katherine accused with a mock glare. "Go on," she coaxed, her grin widening at Rose's groan. "Drink up, bitches!"

I dissolved into a puddle of giggles at the crudeness spilling from Katherine's mouth. The more time I spent around her, getting to know her as an actual human being, rather than the gorgeous, mysterious first-born daughter of the Alpha family, the more I liked her. She was just as real, hilarious, and quirky as my favorite people in the world. It made sense that she had to put on a public face, but it made me happy inside to know that she could feel free enough to drop it around me. I promised myself never to take that trust for granted and to always remain a loyal and steadfast friend to her and her family.

"Ughhh," Rose groaned, wiping her mouth with the back of her hand. "Tequila is disgusting."

"Now who's the grandma?" Daphne mocked, slamming back her latest shot. "You're just a baby!" she said a little too loudly, with a wide grin as she swayed to the music. "You wouldn't have survived law school. When we weren't studying, we were drinking. I think I majored in it my first year."

"Me too!" Katherine agreed with a shake of her head. "Sometimes I have no idea how I managed to pass the bar. Wolf metabolism." She raised a shot glass into the air and shot it like a pro then slammed it on the coffee table upside down.

Each woman grabbed a shot glass, raised it into the air, shouted, "To wolf metabolism!" and tipped it back.

Because the bottle of Patron was empty now, we moved on to the chalet's wine stores, which Katherine assured had been well stocked. The conversation turned to extremely sexy husbands, which led to a viewing of particularly naughty pictures snapped on cell phones, many of which I was sure the man in question would be mortified to know had been shared. Rory, Daniella, and I oohed and awed over each picture, then congratulated each woman on their choice of soulmate.

When they were finished, I flicked through the pictures on my phone and clicked on my favorite. "Avert your eyes, Daniella. Your brother's gorgeous body is about to be ogled." Without waiting, I flashed the ladies whose eyes sparkled with appreciation and whose comments made Daniella squirm and cover her ears with pillows.

"Gross!" she yelled, although her voice was muffled through the pillows.

Daphne patted her on the leg. "It's nothing to be embarrassed about. You got an amazing body, so it's only fair your twin brother has one, too. Don't you think?"

Daniella stared at her considering, her emerald green eyes narrowed in thought. "Yeah," she said slowly, nodding hesitantly at first then exuberantly. "Yeah, that makes sense. But it's still gross."

Daphne laughed, picked up the newest opened bottle of wine, and refilled Daniella's glass. "Then, my dear, the trick is to keep drinking until your brain stops working." She raised her glass and clicked it in salute.

Because my head was spinning pleasantly, and I didn't want to push it beyond that point, I sat back and just enjoyed the company I was in. Beside me on the couch, Rory sat with her legs tucked beneath her and half an empty glass of red wine in her hands.

"Hey," I said quietly, nudging her with my elbow. "What's up? You're being really quiet."

She shrugged. "Just wishing Addison was here, that's all." She leaned into me and shot me a saucy grin. "Look at me, so caught up in my soul mate that I'm turning into a stick in the mud."

Katherine leaned forward, her eyes flashing with interest. "Sorry for eavesdropping, but did you just say you found your soulmate?" She put her glass down on the coffee table and wiggled closer.

Rory blushed, a gorgeous shade of rose that infused her with life. She nodded and glanced down before pulling out her phone and clicking on a picture of Addison. "Yeah," she said, holding up the phone so Katherine could see the picture. "Her name is Addison." For a moment, Rory's chin quivered, then she lifted it with pride and turned the phone to smile at her soulmate's image.

Katherine slid off her chair and knelt on the floor before the couch, reaching for the phone to get a better look. Her eyes went wide in recognition, then turned to me in silent question.

I shook my head. "That's not Adeline," I explained. "It's Addison, her sister."

"Twins?" Katherine asked, then scrolled in on the image to take a better look.

"No," Rory spoke up. "Addison is a year younger, but they're almost identical. Or, they were."

Katherine swallowed and nodded her head. "She's gorgeous. I didn't know Adeline very well, but I had a good impression of her. She was smart and independent, even if she ran with the wrong crowd." Katherine's gaze flickered over to Daniella.

I thought back to the brief time I'd spent with Adeline and the conversations we had. She had been smart, and kind, and I'd begun to think she could have been a friend when her life ended too soon. I clenched my jaw and looked away, blinking rapidly to chase away the tears that threatened to ruin the night. It wasn't easy, spending time with Addison when Adeline's loss was so fresh in my mind, but it was getting easier. I often wondered how hard it was on her to spend time with me.

Katherine handed the phone back to Rory and grinned. “It’s amazing, isn’t it? That bond between soulmates. It’s crazy that you girls are finding your mate so young, though. I was close to my three hundredth birthday when I met Quinn.”

“You don’t think it’s weird that she’s a girl?” Rory blurted, then immediately slapped a hand over her mouth. “Old Ones, I’m sorry, I didn’t mean to say that.”

Katherine shook her head. “Don’t be sorry. I know there are wolves out there who are openly against same-sex soulmates, but for the life of me, I can’t wrap my head around that.” She leaned forward and tapped her finger against her cheek. “I mean, if you’ve experienced that connection, and the way you have zero control over it, then how could you ever think there was a choice involved. One wolf sees and recognizes the other half of their soul in another wolf. Your wolf chose her and hers recognized you. Neither of you made a conscious decision, it’s just what fate had in store for you.” She patted Rory’s leg. “But don’t worry, there are way more people who wouldn’t blink an eye than there are idiots in our world. My cousin Damien and his partner dealt with it early on but, now, they have three children and have cut all the negativity out of their lives. You and Addison will find your way and, if anyone gives you grief, I’ll kick their asses.” She smacked her right fist into her left palm and growled menacingly, then dissolved into laughter.

Rory launched herself off the couch, into Katherine’s arms, nearly upending her glass of wine, which I grabbed in a panic. Katherine caught her and wrapped her arms around Rory's petite body and squeezed as the tears that had glazed my eyes a moment earlier, formed and fell onto my cheeks without shame.

"Well, you know, there is one thing you could do for us now," Rory said a little shyly.

Katherine arched a brow. "What's that?"

"Addison isn't a member of The Sisterhood..." Rory let the sentence hang.

"Ohhh," Katherine murmured, touching her nose with her forefinger. "I got you. That will be rectified immediately. Now, if you ladies will excuse me." She pushed to her feet, swayed for a moment, then stepped free of the seating area. "I'm going to go get more snacks. We need to soak up some of the booze, or they might find six dead women in here in the morning." She headed to the kitchen with a chuckle.

I took the opportunity to set my own glass aside and head to the bathroom to break the seal. I padded across a thick and expensive-looking carpet and opened three doors before finding the bathroom.

On my way back, I stopped into the kitchen to see if Katherine needed any help and found her grating cheese over a tray of nacho chips loaded with spicy ground beef, chopped tomatoes and onions, jalapeño peppers, and corn. I eyed the corn speculatively, eyebrows raised and pointed. "You put corn on nachos?"

Katherine plucked one from the tray and popped it in her mouth. "You don't put corn on nachos?"

I shrugged. "It's nachos. I'll eat it. Is there any sour cream or guacamole here?"

"In the fridge," Katherine gestured, but kept grating. It

was quiet for a moment as I pulled the containers out of the fridge and put them on the counter. Then I felt Katherine's gaze shift and turned to see her watching me. "So," she said conversationally, "how is it, really? Seeing Adeline's face every day? And don't give me an obligatory answer."

I inhaled deeply and measured my words. "It's getting easier. The more I get to know her, the more I see their differences."

Katherine popped another kernel of corn in her mouth and chewed, nodding thoughtfully. "How are the nightmares? Getting worse or the same?"

"The same," I confessed, then disguised a cringe by grabbing a chip and munching on it. It wasn't a lie, not exactly. Katherine didn't know the full extent of my nightmares to begin with, no one did, not even Dalia. I felt the weight of that decision like an anvil on my shoulders, but every time I open my mouth to tell someone, the words just wouldn't come. Instead, my mind would begin to hum loudly, filling with voices I didn't recognize and couldn't drown out. They were indecipherable, too, so I was never sure if they were warning me against sharing or begging me to get help.

"Don't be a hero," Katherine warned, setting her insightful gaze on me. "Grief is a bitch and the only way to cope is to move right through her. Are you still seeing Dr. Mira?" she asked even though I was pretty sure she knew the answer already.

"Yeah. Once a week, like clockwork." I tried not to sound dismissive, but I didn't want to talk about my mental health tonight. Tonight, I wanted to ignore the whispers, eat nachos with corn, have another glass of wine even though my head was already spinning, and have fun with my girls. I opened my mouth to say something to that effect when I heard something that had my eyes going wide and my feet hitting the floor as I raced back to the living room.

Rose, Daphne, Rory, and Daniella shimmied and shook their bodies while singing at the top of their lungs about what they really really wanted. I threw my hands into the air, shouted, "Spice Girls!" and began to sing along. A moment later Katherine danced her way out of the kitchen, singing at the top of her lungs, too.

The song was winding down with each of us hitting it word for word, when Katherine's phone rang. She peeled off from the group and put the phone to her ear, plugging her other one so she can hear. I was having so much fun that I almost missed the way her entire body jerked back rigidly or the way her face went stark white then deep red. The spit dried in my mouth and dread filled my stomach, anchoring me to the floor. No one else noticed, but then two other ring tones interrupted the song and I watched, in horror, as Daphne and Rose went through identical metamorphosis the instant they put their phones to their ears.

Rory and Daniella cheered and clapped, still swinging their hips and swaying their shoulders, as the song clicked off and the sound of panicked voices filtered through their drunken joviality.

Rory moved to my side and reached out to touch my arm, worry and confusion written all over her face. "What happened? What's going on?"

I shook my head, trying to focus on each woman's responses to garner some clue as to what had just happened. I heard words like "dead," "murdered," "assassinated," and "sister."

My legs forgot how to hold me up, so I sat with a thump on the nearest chair and waited, hands folded in my lap, staring silently at Katherine until she lowered the phone and closed her eyes. Her lips moved in a silent prayer.

No one said a word, not until Daphne and Rose clicked off, as well. Then all three women looked at each other with baleful gazes and shook their head in grief.

"What..." Daniella managed to say, before falling silent again. The tension in the room was too high to ignore.

Katherine turned to look at us, huddled together, and opened and closed her mouth several times before words would finally come out. "The new Alphas of Belgium and Slovenia were murdered following their appointment ceremonies. Both were shot in the heart with a silver bullet," she spoke like an android as if even saying the words was too much. Her big blue eyes stared, helplessly out behind thick lashes, that fluttered in confusion.

I gaped as my brain exploded into action, trying to reason out any way that this could've possibly happened without it being what it so obviously was. I sputtered and tried to form a sentence. "Could it have been..." I shook my head, unable to finish my question.

Daphne shook her head slowly, her skin clammy in shock or rage, I wasn't sure. Probably a combination of both since that was what I was feeling. "No," she said, biting the word out. "There was a message left with each of their bodies so there could be no doubt."

I held my breath.

"What did it say?" Rory whispered hoarsely.

Rose lifted her head and looked at us through damp lashes. "*Know your place or die.*"

CHAPTER 12

I stepped back into the living room carrying two tall glasses of ice water and beelined towards Katherine and Daphne, who were each speaking with hushed tones into their phones. Deep lines of worry marred each woman's face and tension had their shoulders riding high and stiff.

"Drink this," I murmured, pressing one glass into Daphne's hands. She glanced up at me, blinking slowly as if trying to place me, then smiled, the briefest whisper of a smile, and took the glass.

"Thank you," she mouthed, taking a sip.

I felt utterly helpless, without anything to offer these women who were caught in the middle of an impossible situation. I made my way across the room to where Katherine paced, wearing out the thick rug beneath her feet.

"Are you sure?" Katherine squeezed her eyes shut and stopped, pressing her hand against her stomach like a woman about to be sick. She swallowed hard and took a deep, steadying breath, then opened her eyes, and met my gaze. "Okay," she whispered, keeping her gaze locked on mine. "Thanks." She turned the phone off and slipped it into her pocket, then accepted the glass I held out.

"Thank you," she murmured after downing half the glass in one gulp.

I waited, silently, knowing she'd share what had obviously been another deep blow when she was ready, and everyone could listen. The pain she was feeling radiated out from every pore in her body and darkened her blue eyes. I laid my hand on her arm and squeezed gently.

"I don't know what to say," I whispered, offering a sad smile when her hand floated up to cover mine. "I don't think there's anything that could be said right now that would make any sense. But whatever you need, I'm here."

Katherine's eyes filled with tears that she quickly blinked away. She was so strong, it always amazed me to see the proof of it. She wasn't cold, she felt things deeply, maybe even deeper than other people, but she was strong enough to keep it together when she had to. I promised myself that if or when I was put in a position of leadership, I would look to her for inspiration and guidance.

"I'd say not to worry about it," Katherine said, blowing out a slow breath. "But that would be dismissive, and you deserve more, Elena." She rubbed her hands over her face, which showed signs of deep fatigue and grief. "The Sisterhood will survive this but those women…" She choked up and had to stop for a moment before continuing. "They were my friends. My mentors. They trusted us to keep them safe and we failed." Her face crumpled and she sat heavily in a nearby chair, then lowered her forehead to her hands.

I sank to my knees and gripped her arms, pulling away so I could see her face. There was so much pain written in her eyes that it stabbed my heart. "Don't you dare do that," I whispered forcefully enough that her eyes went wide in surprise. "Katherine, after the attack on the school you told me repeatedly that it wasn't my fault, that this world is filled with good people who try to do good things. But bad people exist too, and we aren't responsible for what they do." I tightened my grip on her forearms, determined to make her hear me. "Your mother and those women over there," I glanced across the room. "They're going to be feeling the same guilt you do right now. Do you think it's their faults this happened?"

I knew it was a dirty trick, but it was the best way I knew how to pull her out from the darkness that was trying to drag her down. She was strong, yes, but even the strongest women needed help sometimes. It was a measure of their strength that they accepted help.

Katherine swallowed and took a deep breath then nodded once, sharply, and let out a bitter laugh. "You know, it sucks to hear your own words spoken back to you. But you're right, guilt isn't going to help us find justice or understand why." She drank the rest of the water and put the cup down on the coffee table, then pushed to her feet. "Let's gather the troops, then, shall we?"

I nodded and took her offered hand. She tugged me to my feet and reached out and gently cupped my cheek. The sweetness and unexpectedness of the move made my heart ache for my mother. I wondered if she was thinking about her daughter, Eve, now.

"You're so much stronger and braver than I was at your age," Katherine murmured. "You'll be a remarkable woman, Elena."

She turned and walked away without another word, leaving me stunned and half breathless. When she sat at the dining room table and called the group together, I moved on automatic to sit down.

Daphne and Rose joined us last, and sat with heavy sighs, placing their cell phones face down on the table before looking up at Katherine. Each looked exhausted and fragile, but I knew their backbones would hold up against the pressure.

Katherine cleared her throat and placed her hands on the edge of the table. "Three more members of The Sisterhood are missing." She inhaled deeply and blew it out before continuing. "Unlike Elise and Irena, there were no bodies found, but the same note was left in each woman's home. Signs of struggle and injury were found as well." She looked down at her hands and fell silent.

"Who were they?" Rory's question came out as barely a whisper.

"Jacqueline Devante, Lianna Sayles, and Zuri Abioye." Katherine buried her face in her hands and began to quietly weep.

Each name was familiar and came with memories of faces and families and personal stories of friendship told by either Sylvie or Katherine. I saw Katherine shoulders shake as she grieved and felt a surge of hatred and fury towards those responsible.

"What do we do now? How do we make them pay? We need to do something." I curled my fingers into a fist that I pounded against the table. I blinked away tears of sadness, not wanting the fragility of pain. No, I wanted the rage, I embraced it and let it wash over me, sharpening my mind and determination. There was a time for grief, Elise and Irena would be mourned. But, Jacqueline, Lianna, and Zuri were alive or, at least, there was no evidence, yet, that they were dead.

Katherine lifted her head and blinked away tears, looking so much like a lost little girl that it nearly stole my breath to see my hero so fragile. She inhaled deeply and wiped the tears from her cheeks, then sat up and squared her shoulders, moving purposefully. I watched her gather herself, piece by piece, and had to look away to hide the shimmer of pride and awe she inspired in me.

"We don't know who is responsible for this, yet," Katherine said in a flat voice that wavered only slightly. "But we'll find out and they'll pay." She put her hands on the table and pushed to her feet, then exhaled, and sat back down. "Old Ones, I'm sorry. I just thought we were past this." She looked up at Daphne and Rose and shook her head. "Didn't you think we were past this? That all the bad shit was behind us?"

They both nodded in unison.

"It's like a dream," Rose murmured, shaking her head. "Not this." she lifted her hands then let them fall. "It feels like the past year was the dream in this painting and grief is just one more day in my life." She smiled sadly. "I knew it was too good to be true."

Daphne's hand shot out and grabbed Rose's forearm.

"No," she said insistently. "The life you've made with Liam is real and true. You will never be trapped like you were in the mountain, never again!" Daphne tugged, forcing Rose to lift her chin and meet her gaze. "Bad people will always try to hurt those fighting for freedom and equality. They don't get to erase the good."

"Daphne is right," Katherine said. "But I know how you feel, Rose." She swallowed and blinked back more tears. "It feels like we only just got our balance back. After Dad..." Katherine looked away and blew out a deep breath before continuing. "After Dad's murder and everything we went through with Raphael and the Alpha Council, but sometimes felt like the happy moments weren't really real. Like they were the dream and at any second, I could wake up and be back in that barn or at dad's funeral." She licked her lips. "But lately, my life had started to feel real again and now this."

The room was silent for a long moment. The rage I'd tried so desperately to embrace had fizzled out as Rose and Katherine had spoken about the pain of their past. I know exactly how they felt, so much so that hearing my response and emotions spoken aloud by two other women had filled my throat until I wasn't sure I could speak even if I tried.

My life back in Newfoundland hadn't been perfect. There had been ups and downs, family fights and arguments between friends, but I'd been happy and settled. I'd had dreams that were attainable but never far-reaching and solid relationships that made me feel safe and secure.

All of that had changed the moment I'd stepped foot in Alpha Wolf Academy. No, I amended, coming here had just been a necessary step on the path to my understanding of who I really was. Not that I knew who I was, yet, not really. I had a long way to go before that was possible, especially with the revelation of my Alpha powers.

I didn't blame Alpha Wolf Academy even though it would be so easy to project my feelings onto the school. Coming here hadn't caused the pain and chaos, it had just set things into motion. The simplicity and innocence of my life back home had just been a dream, like a gift given to me by my parents and The Sisterhood, even though I didn't always see it that way.

I'd felt so betrayed when I'd first found out and, occasionally, that feeling of helplessness and frustration welled up again and dragged me under. But I'd spent a lot of time thinking about it, about the possible alternatives the sisterhood could have decided on. I could have been raised in seclusion, trained from childhood to take back my rightful place as the Alpha of Russia. I could have been prepared my entire life for the duties that would come with that role.

Instead, I'd been given loving parents and wide-open fields. I'd been given a childhood with memories of scrapes and laughter and hugs and tears that formed me into the person I was now. I'd been gifted with a life, free of grief and the terrible weight of responsibility that sat squarely on my shoulders now. Yes, it sucked to be hit with all of this after twenty-one years of ignorance, but those twenty-one years had been happy and real. The pain of the present couldn't negate the joy of the past.

I wanted to share my thoughts with them, to add my

experiences to the mix and that Rose and Katherine know that they weren't alone in this, but before I could speak a buzz sounded from Katherine's phone, breaking the silence. She lifted it and glanced at the screen, weariness crossing her face before her eyebrows lifted in surprise.

"It's Anthony. Looks like we're being called into a war council." She accepted the video chat and rose from the table, moving across the room swiftly to disappear down the hallway.

Rory pushed to her feet, glancing around the group. "That's our cue to leave, I suppose." She offered Daphne and Rose supportive looks then pushed her chair back and stepped free. "Elena, are you coming with us or do you have to stay?" Her big eyes asked more than she spoke aloud.

I froze with indecision; not sure I was even welcome to stay. I'd been included in a lot of discussions pertaining to The Sisterhood, but this was beyond my pay grade, not that I had a pay grade. I glanced at Daphne and Rose and noted their brief nods.

"I think," I said with a nervous swallow, "I'm going to stay." I got up with Rory and Daniella and fidgeted with my fingers as they gathered their things and headed towards the door.

I felt like an idiot, like a child pretending to be an adult by wearing her mother's lipstick and fancy heels. Inside, not even deep down, I felt like a fraud.

"I don't know why they want me here," I whispered, lifting my gaze to Rory's. I wished I hadn't announced that I would stay, but it was too late for that. "I don't know what I can do to help."

Rory's eyes narrowed her lips firmed. "Like it or not, Elena, you're a part of this world. No one expects you to have all the answers." She smiled softly. "Except for you, that is." She reached out and took my hands, squeezing hard enough to help me find that center of balance it felt like I was always chasing these days. "You belong here and you're stronger than you know. Text when you head out, okay?"

I nodded and squeezed her hands back then glanced over at Daniella who was chewing her lip thoughtfully. "Are you all right with me staying?" *And with you not staying,* I didn't say it aloud but knew we all understood the sub context.

She blinked slowly, looking up in that slow sinuous way she did that I now understood she often used as a stalling technique to give her time to gather her thoughts. I tucked away that little trick in my memory for another day and hoped I could pull it off half as good as she did.

Daniella arched a perfect brow and smiled, the perfect mask to hide her consternation. "Of course," she said lightly. "We'll talk later." She pulled the door open and sailed out, her heels clicking against the wood floor like sharp staccato beats.

I grimaced and shot Rory a disbelieving look. "She's pissed," I murmured beneath my breath, hoping she didn't hear.

"Oh yeah," Rory agreed with a wide grin. "The Queen is used to being at the center of attention and I'm sure it isn't easy on her to play second fiddle to anyone, especially you." With that, she turned and strolled after Daniella, disappearing around the corner of the hallway a moment later, leaving me alone to deal with a situation that was way over my head.

Closing the door, I squared my shoulders and took a deep breath. I might feel like I was drowning but I'd stay afloat no matter what.

By the time I made it back to the dining table, Katherine had returned and she, Daphne, and Rose had set up one of the laptops so that we could all see the other players in attendance at the war council.

Anthony nodded and greeted me by name as I took my place next to Rose. He launched into a detailed description of the crime scenes, including the two murder sites, his face a study in controlled fury as I tore a paper napkin to shreds beneath the table, unable to calm my nerves.

If I were ever going to take my place alongside these players, I would have to up my game.

"... Elena?" I heard my name and a familiar voice and snapped back to attention, focusing in on Sylvie, whose face filled the computer screen. She looked exhausted and expectant, as if I had the only answer to a dire question.

Sylvie nodded encouragingly at me then said in a tone that was decidedly Alpha, "Tell the others what you told me. It might very well be our only clue as to who is responsible for this tragedy."

CHAPTER 13

Flustered, I pulled out my only weapon, unwilling to let a room full of people I admired know that I'd let my concentration drift off during such an important discussion. I lowered my lashes and lifted them, slowly, imitating Daniella, giving myself a few desperate seconds to try to place the question that had been asked of me.

My subconscious came to the rescue, proving some part of my brain had actually been listening after all.

I addressed Sylvie but let my gaze touch briefly on each person in the room as I'd seen Katherine do more than once and tried to sound intelligent. "Just before the plane crash," I said in an even voice, even though the mere thought of the attempt on my life sent a chill up my spine. "Bash and I overheard a conversation between several young men of affluent families, led by Benson Wellington III. He was extremely vocal about his opinion of The Sisterhood as well as his grandfather's hateful attitude towards the women who at that time had stepped forward in roles of authority." I lifted a hand and gestured towards the screen. "His animosity was focused very much on you, Sylvie, and you, Katherine," I added glancing at Katherine.

Ronan frowned. "Did he say anything specific? Reference any plan against The Sisterhood or our family?" He tapped his finger against his bottom lip and waited for an answer.

I thought back to that night, the clear sky and the way I'd felt after being with Bash. We'd felt the bond between us for the first time that night, really felt it, and we'd both been riding on the high of that connection. It's what had driven us out onto the deck, to the hot tub and the promise of fun sexy times.

"Nothing specific," I said slowly, chewing over my words as I replayed the scene again, not wanting to miss anything that might be important. "He spoke about his grandfather having a plan, too," I lifted my fingers on either side of my head and made quotation signs, "make the bitches pay or something to that effect."

Anthony shook his head and made a humming sound deep in his throat. "What do we know of the boy?"

Everyone looked at me expectantly.

"He's an entitled snob who has major issues with authority figures in general and women in particular." I remembered just how hard it had been for him to bend even in the wake of my Alpha voice, but bend he had. I knew everyone on this war council were in the know about my new fancy powers, so I explained, in detail, how he'd attacked me then reluctantly fallen into line once our side had pulled out the big guns. "He might've listened to me after all that, but I could see the endless hate in his eyes when he looked at me."

"Do you think he is intelligent enough or strong enough to have gained his grandfather's approval and confidence? Benson Wellington senior trusts very few people. I'm shocked he trusted his son enough to grace him with the name, let alone a third-generation."

I considered, even though I wanted to jump to conclusions about the ass hat. He wasn't dumb, I knew that, but he led with bravado and brute force, so I had no way to be sure of his intelligence and deviousness. I shook my head. "I don't know him well enough. Bash would, though. Headmistress Donahue, too." The Headmistress struck me as a woman who noticed the truth about people rather than just seeing the gloss they wore like masks.

Sylvie nodded. "Well, while I doubt Wellington would share any real plans he had with his grandson, we do have to look into the possibility that the boy knows more than he divulged. But," she continued, looking directly at me, "if he is wrapped up in whatever that man is planning, we don't want to tip them off. He still has no idea you heard his private conversation, right, Elena?"

I nodded.

"Who were the others he was talking to?"

"Chaz Cartwright and Donavan Boucher," I said immediately, having dredged their names from my memory in anticipation of the question.

Pens scratched on paper, noting down the guys' names. I went back to fidgeting beneath the table.

The conversation moved away from me, thankfully, and onto various other conspiracy theories based on the knowledge they presently had. From what I could gather, The Sisterhood had been frantically pulling in favors and scrambling to round up information on the women who had been murdered and those who had been kidnapped in the hopes of creating a foundation of where to take the investigation.

I'd watched enough episodes of CSI and read enough JD Robb books to know that it was important to know the victim if you wanted to find the perpetrator.

I couldn't help with that side of things; I hadn't known the women personally and wasn't up to date on the social or political fine points of our society. I'd been taking lessons from Sylvie for months now, but there is just too much history to cover to have a firm grasp on it so soon. My frustration searched for something I could contribute and landed firmly on Benson Wellington III.

I was the only one here that had a personal connection to him. He hated me with the fiery passions of hell, which meant he probably wouldn't be very gracious, but that didn't mean I couldn't get something out of him. Sylvie had mentioned the danger of tipping off the grandfather by poking into Benson's involvement, but surely, I could get something out of the asshole without raising any red flags. I turned the idea over in my mind, considering how I could stage a run in that would look innocent. I didn't know much about him beyond the fact that he'd threatened Rory more than once and was a world-class shit, but I had friends who would have the whole scoop on him.

It made me feel useful, the thought that I could potentially contribute something more to the cause. When all eyes had been on me, waiting for information only I could give, I'd felt pressure and nerves, which had made me feel nauseous, but even that had been better than the feeling of uselessness I had sitting here. I looked around the table and at the people on the computer screen and wondered how they did it. There was pain, and fear, and unimaginable anger in each of them, but they were all business now. Even Rose, who'd never been trained to be a member of an Alpha family, was ready and able to focus all the negative energies in the room on the single goal of finding justice for those women.

My mind wandered again, slipping away from the present to skim over my memories of the last year. Like Rose, I hadn't had the training Sylvie, Katherine, and the LaFlamme men had. Even Daphne, who'd been born and raised in Newfoundland, like me, had spent the last decade of her life working alongside Jacob Little Foot, honing her skills in the face of stress and urgency. I studied Rose in the way she leaned into the table, engaging in the conversation, her face alight with passion and razor-sharp focus.

She'd found her place in this world, obviously, while I was still struggling to get my feet under me. *Fake it till you make it*; I repeated my personal mantra in my head and forced my attention back to the topic at hand.

"There's not a whole lot we can do until we get those reports in," Anthony said with a frown that made him look even more like his deceased father. I wondered if it was comforting to Sylvie to see so much of her late husband, the previous Alpha of Canada, Pierre LaFlamme, in her eldest son. It had been the furthest thing from comforting to see my eyes looking out at me from my psychotic uncle's face.

"Okay," Sylvie said with finality that indicated the end of this war council. "We each know what we have to do. Katherine," she added. "Your transport should be there soon. I'll see you, Rose, and Daphne soon and boys," she addressed her sons, each Alphas in their own right. "We'll meet again tomorrow with updates and, hopefully, some good news." Her screen went blank, followed immediately by Anthony's, Ronan's, and Tegan's. Katherine closed the laptop and scanned the faces at the table.

"You heard the boss," she said with a soft smile that didn't quite reach her eyes. "Let's grab our things and meet the chopper." Katherine glanced at me and blinked, as if just registering that I was still here.

The acid in my stomach bubbled to life.

"Elena," she said, pushing up from the table and gathering her notes. "I know this is a lot, but it's good that you were here. We're not going to cut you out of the loop, I promise. You'll be included in our meetings. Are you alright with that?"

I swallowed and nodded, then added, "yes," when I realized she wasn't looking at me. She had a lot more than me on her mind, so I didn't blame her. I resolved to face down Benson and pull something useful out of his moronic brain so this overwhelming feeling of uselessness would ease up, even just a little.

I stepped back, out-of-the-way, and watched as the three women gathered their things as quickly as possible and headed for the door, then nodded at each of them and murmured," stay safe," before turning towards my dorm so I could rope my friends and mate into an undercover operation.

And stopped dead when I saw Connor waiting for me at the end of the hallway.

CHAPTER 14

"What the hell are you doing here?" I snapped, immediately going on the offensive. The last time I'd seen him, he'd been concussed and had kissed me. I bit back the rest I wanted to snarl because his concussion had been my fault.

He cocked an eyebrow in a way I'd once found irresistible but now found incredibly annoying.

"Suck it up, Princess," he clapped back, surprising me. "The Sisterhood is under attack and they don't need anything else added to their already extremely full plate. You will stay out of trouble," he took a step closer and leveled his icy blue eyes on me. "I'll make damn sure of it."

My breath caught in my chest as he stalked closer, his lips pressed tightly together. He looked like a predator.

I could use a predator to keep me safe.

It took effort to swallow my pride, but I did. He was right. Viktor would certainly take this opportunity to plan an attack on my life. Dread shivered up my spine at the realization that the war council had missed a possible angle on the attacks. What if Viktor had staged them so he could use the upheaval to his benefit?

"Thank you," I said, looking him straight in the eye. It didn't feel forced, not now that I'd made that connection. And once I spoke to Sylvie about my fears, she'd agree that Connor was a necessary evil. It was time to put the past behind us and move the fuck on. "Sorry about slamming you up against a cave." I moved past him, heading towards my dorm and my next step in this undercover op.

He fell into step beside me, never breaking stride, and murmured, "Sorry for kissing you."

♀ ♀ ♀

I wasted no time in calling Sylvie to inform her of my realization and wasn't in the least shocked when she confessed it was a possibility they were already looking into.

I called Bash but repeatedly got his message. He'd made plans to hang with his friends tonight after I'd gotten the call for The Sisterhood meeting, so I figured they were still out, or he was passed out after drinking way too much. I chewed on my lip and kept walking, wondering if I should postpone the mission until he was able to join.

No, I argued with my instincts. This "accidental run in" only worked if it seemed casual and nothing tipped Benson off to our purpose. Having Bash there would only spike the testosterone levels and start a fight. Benson underestimated me, being a simple woman, even though he knew of my gift. It would be far easier to weasel information out of him without another male around.

I wasn't sure what to do about Connor, but I'd figure it out on the way.

Next, I called Rory, but when she didn't answer. So, I called Daniella and asked her to meet me outside her dorm. I didn't stop moving or planning or ignoring Connor. He'd wanted me to react to that little snide comment and I wasn't going to give him the satisfaction. So, instead, I focused on my goal of rattling Benson's cage until something came loose.

Connor slid into the shadows as we approached the building, probably checking for attackers, hiding in the bushes. I ignored him and walked up to Daniella who was waiting on a bench outside her dorm building, typing something into her phone. She looked up with a bored expression on her perfect face, which was still fully made up, even though she'd changed out of her party clothes into a pair of jeans topped with a fitted and expensive looking jacket.

"I didn't expect you to be finished so quickly," she said, pushing up to her feet. "What little covert affair are you pulling off at this time of the day?" Daniella glanced up at the rising sun and glared as if it offended her.

Since neither of us had gotten any sleep, I understood the reaction.

"Yeah," I said with a shrug. "I mean you don't have to help if you don't want to." I turned slightly away, sure she wouldn't give up an opportunity to work for The Sisterhood, even if it meant working through me.

I wasn't wrong. I'd only taken a single step forward when Daniella sighed.

"Alright," she said as if she were doing me some grand favor. "I'm in. Nothing better to do around here anyway."

Just then Connor reappeared beside me like a ghost, stealing Daniella's attention. She glanced at him then away, then shifted to take a closer look. Her eyes narrowed and something flashed in their emerald depths.

"You must be the infamous Connor," Daniella said, cocking an eyebrow and tilting her head to the side to assess him. Her long, slow appraisal from his boots to the tip of his hair was judgmental as fuck and made me smile. We might not always get along when it was just the two of us, but whenever we were up against anyone else, Daniella had my back.

Connor waited until Daniella had sized him up good then grinned that slow, sideways grin that used to melt my knees. I'm not sure what it did to Daniella's knees, but it made her mouth fall open just a little.

"And you must be the Queen bitch," Connor replied, without breaking eye contact or giving any hint of emotion in his tone.

Daniella's chin lifted and the corners of her lips twitched then fell as she assumed a haughty glare. Anyone who didn't know her would have been immediately intimidated, but I saw the amusement dance behind her eyes and nearly groaned.

I looked back and forth between the two of them, annoyed by whatever was going on and made a dismissive sound. "Okay," I drew the word out to get their attention.

"Bash and Rory are off somewhere not answering their phones, so it's just us."

"And what exactly is the mission, 007?" Daniella said haughtily, finally turning her gaze back to me.

I smiled, liking her reference to James Bond. "The mission, should you choose to accept it, is to intercept Benson Wellington III in a completely natural looking way so that I can interrogate him without him realizing." I set my hands on my hips jauntily and grinned.

Daniella just stared at me. "You want me to start a fight so you can wrangle some information out of him?"

"Yup," I replied.

"Exactly what information do you need to get out of him?" Daniella asked, turning to walk down one of the paths. "His dorm is this way." She glanced back at Connor as I fell into stride next to her.

I considered the fact that Daniella and Rory hadn't been included in the war council but came to the immediate conclusion that they were as trustworthy with my secrets as anyone could possibly be. I could and would share every detail with them and Bash, and, I reluctantly admitted to myself, Connor. There was no use denying the fact that he was back, so he might as well be useful.

"Back before the plane crash," I started, knowing Daniella hated to talk about it but needing to give the conversation context. "Bash and I overheard Benson chatting with Chaz Cartwright and Donavan Boucher about The Sisterhood. Turns out Benson's grandfather is pretty important and has some serious hate for anyone not an old male wolf drowning in money. He made some insinuations that his grandfather had shared some plans to take

The Sisterhood down a few notches. We're just going to go poke around a little without being obvious just in case he actually is wrapped up in something sinister and reports back to his grandfather." I shrugged. "It's more a mission to find out if he's ignorant or involved."

Daniella was silent for a long moment and blew out a deep breath. "Okay, so the challenge is to get him bragging about his importance in his grandfather's life so that he confirms or denies that he'd have information in the first place?"

I chuckled. "Basically. I figure with his superiority complex and how much he despises me, it'll be easy to provoke him to the point where he talks out of his ass. Plus, you're pretty good at pissing people off. You do your thing and I'll do mine." Just to make sure she knew I was joking, kind of, I bumped my shoulder into hers and grinned.

Daniella shot me a glare that was clearly amused than looked at the screen of her cell phone and winced. "You know I didn't sleep at all last night, right?" To punctuate her question, she yawned behind her hand

I understood why she hadn't been able to sleep. The horrific reality of what had happened to our Sisters would've kept anyone awake. I thought of the uselessness I'd felt during the meeting and even now and felt sorry for her.

"I know. I don't think I would've been able to sleep even if I'd gone back to my dorm room. I just need to do something, you know?" I knew she'd understand.

Daniella nodded. "Well, Benson usually has breakfast with his stooges right about now then he goes for a run.

His buddies prefer picking things up and putting them down, so they go to the gym. It will be the perfect time to accidentally run into him." She made quotation marks on either side of her head.

"How do you know so much about them?" I asked, not sure I can remember my own schedule as well as she'd laid out Benson's.

Daniella shrugged. "I just have a knack for recalling details."

"You should join the Men in Black, then," I quipped as we approached the cafeteria. My stomach rumbled at the thought and smell of food and I wished I'd had the fore-thought to have breakfast or coffee before venturing out to 007 the hell out of Benson.

Daniella whirled around and stared at Connor, her eyes blazing. "What did you say?"

I gaped, having been lost in thought so much that I hadn't heard him say anything. Daniella's eyes glinted with wild emotion that I found more than a little surprising. She barely knew Connor. Maybe she was just projecting my annoyance of him like a good friend, which she was steadily becoming more of each day.

Connor crossed his arms over his chest and stood, hips apart, staring down at Daniella. I narrowed my eyes at them, wondering why they were being so weird. It was like watching feral cats face off against each other, all posturing, and hisses.

"I heard you mutter something under your breath," Daniella said sharply, not backing down for even a moment. "What did you say?" She jutted her chin forward and put her hands on her hips. The air practically thickened between them.

Connor moved forward, ever so slightly, putting his face close to hers and murmured, "I said you'd make the black suit look good."

I stood back, feeling like an idiot or a voyeur, and eyed them. They were being weird, and we didn't have time for it. I cleared my throat and stepped forward to push Connor back a full step. He went easily enough but kept his gaze locked on Daniella's.

"Well, that was fun," I said derisively, stepping between them so Daniella's gaze snapped to mine. "Are you ready or do you want to square off a bit longer?"

She blinked, refocusing her eyes on me, then huffed out a breath and stepped around me. "Come on. We don't want to miss out on our chance."

"Okay," I mumbled, rushing to catch up with her quick strides. I shot dagger eyes back at Connor and got a haughty look in return.

Just as Daniella had predicted, Benson and his friends left the cafeteria around ten minutes later and split up. We'd moved past the cafeteria building into the shadows of one of the mature elms, so he'd walk directly into us, thereby igniting the authentically bitter words we'd share. As discussed, Connor faded away, leaving just us girls to our evil devices and wiles.

Benson strode down the path with his head bent to his phone, ignoring everyone and everything around him, which worked perfectly for a plan. My skin jittered with anticipation as I ran the prompts I'd prepared to start this fight over and over in my mind. We had to be careful, so careful. If Benson was caught up in whatever his grandfather and his old cronies had planned, if that was anything at all, then he'd pick up on my suspicion a lot easier.

I'd gone over our bickering and outright fighting after the plane crash and was certain he'd have prodded me or Daniella with some kind of snide comment if he had actual chops to back up his bragging. But he resorted to posturing and general asshole behaviors, which meant one of two things; either he knew nothing at all, or he knew too much and was being careful.

We waited until he was around fifteen feet away and started down the path towards him, chatting about the upcoming party just to make the run in as authentic as possible. We split at the last moment to let Benson walk between us, but not far enough apart to let it happen without bumping shoulders.

His roar of insult was immediate. How dare anyone get in his way? But when he saw who it was that had walked into him, disturbing his peace, his face went dark purple with annoyance and anger.

"Watch where you're fucking going!" he snapped, curling his lips back in a sneer.

I turned my back on him as if to walk away, knowing that would infuriate him much more than standing up to him. Benson didn't deal well with being ignored and it was better for him to think he'd instigated the argument. He'd be less likely to link our probing that way.

"Don't turn your back on me!" he shouted, snaking out a hand to grab my arm. His fingers pressed in my flesh, bruising it. I thanked the Old Ones our kind healed quickly. There would be no evidence of his presumption on my body soon enough. He yanked me forward and I let myself stumble, off-balance, while Daniella played her part with a quiet growl.

"Get your hand off her!" Daniella ordered, stepping forward to bare her teeth at Benson. I felt a swell of pride in my chest at the fierceness in her eyes. I knew she was just playing a part right now, but that fierceness wasn't faked. Daniella had my back despite any issues we still had with each other.

Benson dismissed her immediately and turned his gaze on me. Soft voices, like the conversation of several people in a nearby room, whispered urgently in my mind. I focused on pushing them down just like I'd been practicing and narrowed my eyes at my bully.

"That's alright, Daniella. I don't mind." I locked my gaze on his and stepped even closer. "It's not like I haven't beaten him before. It's not like I haven't driven him to his knees, begging for mercy, before."

His eyes went impossibly dark with barely controlled fury but in them I saw a flicker of memory and fear. His hand loosened from my arm and he shoved me back away from him with a growl of disgust.

"You're a freak."

He kept his words low, barely above a whisper, because our little altercation had started to draw eyes as I knew it would. Benson cared about optics almost as much as he cared about dominating others, so those extra eyes would ensure he'd have to come out on top. He wouldn't back down now.

I smiled slowly, letting my eyes fill with amusement and dismissal. "No, what I am is stronger than you." I had advanced forward. "What I am is smarter than you." Another step closer, crowding him, pushing him so his control would snap. "What I am is more important than you."

I saw the moment he snapped and barely held back a grin. Checkmate.

He leaned into me, putting his face so close I could smell the coffee he drank with breakfast and feel the warmth of his breath on my face. It ignited the voices until they rang in my mind, urgent and confusing, a jumble of sound and need and emotion.

I bit back a gasp and pushed through the cacophony inside my head to focus on what I was doing. I prayed Benson didn't notice the effort it took for me to come back to reality and pushed away the fear that tightened my chest painfully. The voices had never been this loud or insistent before. I didn't know what they wanted, and I couldn't push them back like I've been doing. I gritted my teeth and pushed through them, unwilling to show any sign of weakness in front of an enemy.

"You have no fucking idea who I am, little wolf," he snarled.

My heart caught at his use of the same nickname my uncle had used just before he'd tried to kill me, the first time.

Benson's teeth ground together so that he spoke through them, a furious growl. "You're nothing. Your friends are nothing." He glanced hatefully at Daniella and his lips peeled back to reveal a terrifying smile that knew way too much. "Little girls should learn to keep their mouths shut or someone will shut it for them." He thrust his chin forward as if to headbutt me and, instinctively, I flinched, which made his eyes flare with satisfaction. Then he turned on his heels, confident he'd won, and strode away, head high, shoulders back, and hands curled into tight fists.

My head resonated with whispers that layered one on top of the other until the world around me faded away and all I knew was the voices. They pulled at me, trying to drag me down into a darkness I didn't understand but knew would swallow me whole. I fought back, trying to resurface, trying desperately to silence them. My sight went dark.

"Elena!" Daniella shook me by the shoulders and shouted into my face, dragging me into the shadows of a tree.

I heard her, her voice distinct amidst the chaos and focused all my energy on getting to her. Her hands on my shoulders felt like anchors to the real world so I concentrated on them, too, and the feel of the earth under my shoes. I dragged oxygen into my lungs and slowly brought myself back from the edge.

My eyesight returned in a wash of brilliant light and color that made my eyes dampen. Through the tears I saw the fear and desperation on Daniella's face and my heart squeezed sharply in my chest.

"I'm okay," I whispered, hoarsely, nodding assuredly to her and to Connor, whose face loomed just over Daniella's shoulder, pale with worry.

But I wasn't okay. I knew it and, now, they knew it, too.

CHAPTER 15

"You nearly blacked out, Elena," Daniella hissed as she nearly ran to keep up with my long strides. "You are not okay. What happened back there?"

"I'm fine," I muttered, not wanting to delve into the specific details of my mental deficiency right now. I thought quickly about possible excuses for practically losing my mind and settled on one I knew she'd let drop. It was a dirty trick, but I needed a way out. I hesitated, slowing my steps, and turned to catch her gaze. "It was like I was back on the plane..." I bit my lip, feeling horrible for dredging up that trauma, especially when I saw her eyes filled with understanding.

She nodded, barely a movement of her head, and murmured, "I get them, too." She pushed her hands into her jean pockets and fell silent.

Students swarmed past us, on their way to breakfast or early classes, completely oblivious to the drama we'd instigated or the lies I told. I remembered making the decision to trust Daniella with all my secrets and had to swallow back the guilt. I'd tell her, eventually.

Maybe.

This wasn't like the other secrets. It wasn't as if we were all wrapped up in this together, sisters to the end, fighting side-by-side to take down the bad guys. I was going crazy, just like Dalia had, and one day, hopefully not soon, I'd tip over the edge and hurt somebody.

It was my deepest fear. Not that Viktor would find me, torture me and, ultimately kill me. Not that somehow, I'd defeat my uncle and find myself in a position of leadership that I wasn't prepared for. The pressure of those possibilities weighed down on me endlessly, but they weren't what pulsed in the center of my soul every moment of every day since the whispers had begun and Dalia had revealed what they meant.

She'd lost control and hurt innocent children, *her* children. She hadn't known why, but I did, which she assured me meant my experience would be different than hers. I hoped to the Old Ones she was right. She'd learned to control her wild natural powers with time and training, so I could do the same. Then again, to get the help I needed, I'd have to admit that I was hearing the voices already, and I wasn't ready to be locked away quite yet.

"Listen, I know you're tired, I am, too. So, why don't you head back to your dorm room and get some sleep. I'm going to go find Bash and fill him in on the details." I gave her a tired smile and hoped she'd take the hint. I really did need to be alone with my soulmate.

She watched me for a second then nodded. "Okay." She stifled a yawn. "Old Ones, I really want some coffee, but it will keep me awake and I feel like the walking dead." Daniella glanced over at Connor. "You'll make sure she's all right?" Clearly, she was still concerned about me despite my explanation.

"Always," Connor murmured.

Daniella stared at him for a long moment, then nodded again. "Okay. I trust you. And you," she said pointing a finger at me with a devilish smile, "don't even think about waking me up before noon."

"Deal." I didn't tell her that I planned on sleeping until mid-afternoon. I turned and headed towards Bash's dorm with Connor following at a distance.

I let myself into Bash's room with the key he'd given me months ago and saw his bed rumpled and obviously slept in. The smell of whiskey in the air confirmed my suspicions that his night out with the guys had gotten lush. I followed the trail of discarded clothes to the shower and watched him lean into the spray of hot water with his eyes closed.

He was gorgeous. I was always slightly surprised by how much the beauty of him affected me. The fact that he was my soulmate was beyond comprehension and I thanked the Old Ones every day that they'd blessed me with his love. Without making a sound, I pulled my clothes off, leaving them puddled on the floor, and pulled the shower door open.

"Looks like my day is about to get a hell of a lot better," Bash murmured, finally opening those emerald green eyes to look at me. His hand slid around my waist and tugged me forward.

My body fit against his so perfectly. I leaned into his

embrace, wrapping my arms around his neck thrusting my fingers into his wet black hair to draw him near. He tasted of the whiskey with hints of saltiness that made me want to nibble and bite.

So, I did.

He moaned beneath my lips and tilted his head for a better angle as his hands dipped low over the curve of my body, then slid, inch by inch, up until his thumbs brushed over the peaks of my nipples. I arched into his hands, breaking our kiss to release a sigh of pleasure. His mouth found my skin and moved deliciously over its surface, leaving trails of fire in his wake. I hung on, head fallen back, as he devoured my neck and shoulders, then grasped my hips and lifted me until my legs wrapped around his waist and my back was pressed against the tile wall.

His mouth fit over my nipple and his teeth bit sharp, almost painfully, around the sensitive peak. I cried out and dug my nails into the skin of his neck, lost in the twin sensations of pain and pleasure.

Steam built around us, locking us into a magical mist where only we existed. I let my mind drift in the events that weighed so heavy on me, faded away for the moment. My body writhed, begging for more, bucking my hips against him as he drove me closer to oblivion with each lick or bite.

Pressure built between my thighs, exquisitely painful, perfectly sensual, making me squirm and murmur incoherent demands until Bash slipped his hand between us and soothed my ache with his fingers.

My body shook as I came abruptly, shattering into

pieces as he rocked his palm against me and moved his fingers in and out, in and out. Then he was shifting and it was all I could do to hold on and breathe as he filled me and began to move.

My world burst with color as he drove me up again, too fast, too hard to prepare for the explosion that rocked me from head to toe and deeper still. I cried out as my inner muscles twitched, holding him tight within me as he came with a roar and his body sagged against mine.

We stayed like that, me trapped between Bash's satiated body and the tile wall of the shower as water, no longer hot, beat down on us. I could've stayed like that forever but when the water changed from warm to freezing cold, we screamed in unison and bolted out.

I stood naked in the middle of his bathroom shivering, my blood rushing wildly through my veins as my skin pebbled in response to the cold. I accepted the towel he handed me and wrapped it around my body, stifling a yawn.

"How can you be tired after that?" Bash asked with a laugh. He raked his hands through his wet hair, then over the stubble on his chin as he glanced in the mirror. "Ugh-hh," he grumbled. "I'm going to have to shave or risk looking like a homeless man." He reached for his shaving cream, then paused when his gaze met mine in the mirror.

Bash turned, uncaring of the fact that he was completely nude. "What's wrong?" He crossed the bathroom to me and reached for my hand. My fingers closed over his and held on as he gathered me into his arms.

I shook. My entire body began to tremble as he held me softly against his chest, murmuring softly to calm me down. I squeezed my eyes shut and tried to force myself to find the balance one last time, but I'd pushed too far already and my soul knew I was in a safe place. I gave in to the exhaustion and cascade of emotions that I'd held back since hearing of the murders. Bash gathered me in his arms, as easily as a parent lifts the child, and walked me out of the bathroom and over to his bed.

I curled onto his lap and let the tears come.

After a while, I felt the press of his mind on mine, asking to be let in so he could understand. I felt his confusion and worry as if it were my own and opened to him immediately. Without words, I told him everything that happened, from the news, to the war council, to Connor's return, and our planned encounter with Benson. He held me and rocked, soothing one hand down the length of my spine until my eyes grew heavy and I drifted into sleep.

♀ ♀ ♀

I drifted out of dreams plagued by faceless murderers to the delectable scent of bacon and maple syrup.

My eyelids were heavy. I squeezed them shut and yawned widely and arched my back in a spine crunching stretch that released a good bit of the tension that had been lingering in me while I slept.

"Come on," Bash coaxed, settling onto the bed next to me and lightly tracing the contour of my face with his fingertips. "I may or may not have bribed one of the cooks into making you breakfast for supper."

I peeked at him, so handsome and caring, then at the plate in his hand and drooled. My stomach, which hadn't seen food since early the night before, grumbled loudly, making my mate chuckle. He moved the plate away so I wouldn't topple it as I sat up and placed a pillow on my lap. With greedy hands I reached for the food, shimmying my shoulders in anticipation.

"Why do girls do that?" Bash asked, a frown creasing his brow.

"Do what?" I asked around a piece of bacon that was making my mouth water.

Bash linked his hand towards me. "That dance, with your shoulders. Every girl I know does that when someone brings her food."

I made a rude dismissive sound and shook my head. "I don't do that."

"You just did it." Bash looked at me and mimicked my shimmy.

My eyes went wide in recognition. "Crap, I do that all the time." I frowned, trying to remember what my girlfriends did when presented with food and had to bite back a laugh. "Okay, but it can't be all girls. I can't see Daniella doing it, or your mom." My eyes got even wider and I said on a gasp, "Old Ones, I think Sylvie LaFlamme does it!"

It felt good to laugh, even if it was at my own expense. The darkness of the night before lifted just a little with each moment I spent with Bash. My chest ached in a good way at the intensity of love I felt for him in that moment. I lifted a piece of bacon to his lips as an offering and smiled when he nipped it from my fingers.

"So, now that you're fed and rested, we should probably talk about what happened," Bash said, reaching for the twin to-go coffee cups. He handed me one and waited until I'd taken a long sip followed by an appreciative moan, to put it back on the nightstand.

I chewed my lip for a second, trying to remember what I'd shared with him before passing out in his arms. It was all a little hazy, as I'd been exhausted, physically and emotionally. Plus, there'd been that little deal with the voices in my head. "I'm sorry, I was really tired. I thought I shared everything with you before I fell asleep."

"No, you did. It's getting really clear between us, the connection, almost like watching a movie or playback, except I also experience your emotions while it happens to you. Did you know that?" He poked at a rip in his jeans absently.

I thought about the times he'd shared things with me and flushed at the memory of the extremely dirty promises he'd made just the other day. There had been significant detail in his imaginative description and, just like it had the first time, it made my skin heat and my body react.

"Ummm..." I said around a piece of pancake covered in maple syrup in my mouth, using the food and as an excuse to calm my hormones. This wasn't exactly the time for sex.

Bash chuckled softly. "I'm not talking about that, although, maybe I am." He rubbed a hand over his chin, which I noticed had been shaved since that morning. "It's days later and you're still reacting to that little message I sent. I don't think it's because it was particularly raunchy, although," he arched an eyebrow, "I am particularly proud of the level of raunch. But I was really horny when I sent it. Like, over the top, about to explode, horny. I think, maybe, that's why it affected you so much. You experienced my emotions."

I considered his theory for a moment, then nodded. "That makes sense. It was like being hit with lightning, like going from zero to sixty in three seconds. One minute I was sitting in class, listening to a lecture on the physiology of wolves, and the next minute I was practically in When Harry Met Sally!"

Bash's face turned purple as he pressed a hand against his mouth, trying to hold back the laughter that bubbled up from his gut and burst free no matter what he did.

I smacked him, hard. "It's not funny! It was really embarrassing. Everyone knew exactly what I was feeling. I had to run out of class. I am not sure I can ever show my face in there again." I closed my eyes and shook my head. "And Mr. Talbot! He's so old and musty. His face was just... I could've killed him!"

Bash grabbed his stomach and keeled over, laughing so hard he couldn't speak. I grabbed the closest thing to me, another pillow, and bashed him over the head with it, but that just made him laugh harder. So, I glared at him and finished my breakfast, not offering him a single morsel of what was left out of sheer spite.

I drank my coffee while he collected himself, then commandeered his because he'd made me relive the embarrassment of this little experiment. We'd already discussed what had happened, in length, while I'd still been freshly mortified and we each agreed to only sending sexy messages when we knew the other was in a safe space. I tossed the second empty coffee cup into the wastebasket and made my way to Bash's bathroom to freshen up.

I felt like a new woman when I emerged, half an hour later, showered and groomed, and dressed in one of his T-shirts, which I'd nabbed on my way in.

Bash was sitting at his computer desk and swiveled around in his chair to face me. Instead of the smile that had been there when I'd gone into the bathroom, his lips were tight, and he looked troubled.

"What's wrong?" I settled on the edge of the bed and faced him.

He took a deep breath and exhaled it slowly, making my stomach muscles jitter with nerves. Nothing good ever came from a laborious exhalation.

"I just…" He rubbed his chin and sighed again. "Before we started laughing earlier, I wanted to talk about last night, but then we got a little sidetracked."

Part of me wanted to crack a joke and lighten the mood, but I could feel the tension through our bond and see it in his face. Whatever he needed to say, I would listen. So, I nodded and waited for him to find the words.

A muscle worked in his jaw and Bash stood up from his chair and began pacing the room, letting a little of the wildness inside him peek out. The reticence I now realize had been present in the way he'd spoken and moved earlier, faded away now and was replaced by an intensity that made me shiver.

I reached out a hand, then pulled it back when he whirled around, emerald eyes glinting, and growled at me.

CHAPTER 16

My eyes went wide in surprise and I just stared at my soulmate, unable to find words through my shock.

This wasn't like him. Bash was sweet, and sexy, smart, and patient. He was everything I could've ever hoped for in a mate and I'd rarely seen him react so strongly to anything except when Viktor had been trying to kill me. I'd seen the wildness in him then, and it had thrilled me to know that he'd fight for me.

I wasn't in imminent danger now, though, but still, Bash's eyes glittered with anger, making my stomach churn. My fingers dug into the bedspread as I frantically tried to figure out why he was so mad, especially when he'd been laughing with me not that long ago.

"We're a team," Bash said in a low voice, looking up at me through thick lashes. "We're mates, but last night you acted like a lone wolf. Worse," he lifted his head and glared, "You took another man with you, instead of me.

How exactly did you think that would make me feel, Elena?"

My mouth fell open and I blinked slowly, trying to wrap my head around it. "You're angry I went to see Benson without you?" I saw the way his hands clinched and unclenched in the muscle that worked in his jaw and understood that yes, he was angry I'd gone to see Benson without him. "But I called you. You know I did. You were out with the guys or passed out. And I'm not saying there's anything wrong with that, you didn't know."

"That's the point! I didn't know. You found out that two women were murdered and three more abducted, and you didn't tell me right away." He got up and began pacing the room, like a caged animal. "You thought that maybe Benson might know something about it all and went to confront him without me."

I sputtered. "You didn't answer your phone..."

"And you couldn't have waited?" He pivoted and threw up his hands. "You had to confront someone possibly involved in that kind of atrocity and you couldn't wait a few hours for me to fucking wake up?" His voice boomed from his chest.

Excuses bubbled to my tongue, desperate to be pleaded, but I bit them back. I hated to admit it, but he was right. I'd been exhausted and emotionally distraught, yet I'd dragged Daniella and Connor across campus to stage a provocation. I could have waited; it should have waited. My chest ached with regret but before I could say anything, he continued his rant.

"Sylvie specifically said to leave it alone, in case

Benson is involved which, from what he said is a probability. So, you directly disobeyed your Alpha and dragged my sister into it with you. Did you even think about that?" Bash thrust his hands into his hair, gripping his head as if it were about to explode. He was so worked up I didn't think he'd heard me. So, I said it again.

His mention of Daniella tipped my internal scales from regret to annoyed so fast it made my head spin. "Your sister is a big girl, Bash," I said with a frown. "She can make her own decisions." I hadn't forced her to do anything.

His eyebrows shot up, widening his eyes. "So, you're saying she would've gone off and done it on her own, then?" That muscle worked in his jaw again.

"No," I spat out. "But you weren't there, Bash. You said that you experienced hearing about those women through me, through my emotions, yet you're acting like I just flew off the handle and went rogue!" Frustration churned violently in my gut.

"Didn't you, though?" he questioned, resuming his pacing. "What else do you call it when you directly ignore the command of your Alpha?"

I opened my mouth to retort, then snapped it shut when everything I'd wanted to yell at him suddenly made no sense. I'd fucked up, I realized, with an overwhelming sinking feeling. I'd have to tell Sylvie, let her know my suspicions about Benson's involvement. I pressed a hand to my stomach as if it would somehow, magically, hold back the nausea.

The tension in the room was so sick, it made my skin

buzz, and not in the good way that Bash usually made me buzz. I grasped for the words to apologize, to explain why I'd felt the need to do something, to not sit idly by with nothing to offer when everyone around me was being torn to shreds.

I reached out to him through our bond, needing him to understand that my intentions hadn't been selfish, even if they'd been misguided and colored by exhaustion and grief.

But I couldn't feel him or his emotions, I realized. I frowned and reached out again, searching for the connection between us.

It wasn't there. The open path between us wasn't there no matter how hard I reached for it. Panic throbbed like bright flames at the base of my skull. He was shutting me out.

I pushed my feet and stood on shaky legs, half of me wanting to cry while the other half wanted to fight.

Bash caught the movement and paused in his frenetic pacing to stare at me. There must've been something in my expression to give away how appalled and hurt I felt, because his shoulders slumped forward and he dug his hands into his jeans pockets, glancing away for a moment.

"How could you..." I sputtered as heat rushed to my face, making me feel lightheaded.

Two knocks sounded on the door, courtesy only, before opening to reveal Daniella, Rory, and Connor, who peered in with a look of concern wrinkling his forehead.

I gritted my teeth and moved to the door to usher in my friends, even though they'd come at the worst possible time, and slammed the door behind them. But, before I could manage the move, Bash called out, "Connor, why don't you come in? You're as much a part of this as any of us." Bash tilted his head, stiffly, inviting my ex into his dorm room.

I turned away from Connor and shot Bash a searing glare that didn't help dissipate the tension in the air. I wondered briefly how Daniella and Rory could walk into it without feeling it. The tension moved through the room, filling my body, drawing out the whispers.

Rory settled on Bash's bed and settled one of the pillows on her lap. "Sorry I wasn't around this morning," she said. "I was over at Addison's and my phone was on mute, so I didn't hear it." A slight blush pinked her cheeks, making it clear to anyone in the room who was paying attention that Rory had missed out on the mornings fun because she'd been having a sexy sleepover with her girlfriend. "Daniella said that you guys went to talk to Benson..." Rory let the sentence trail off, not quite a question but definitely questioning.

"Yeah," I replied, turning away from Bash to talk to my friend. "I know you guys felt like shit when you left, and it wasn't any better for me." I ran a hand through my hair as if that could somehow magically soothe the voices, so they went back to sleep or whatever it was they did when I wasn't agitated. "Everyone at that table had something to do, a part to play in finding justice for those women, but..." I lifted my hands and let them fall to my side uselessly.

"But you felt useless, so you did the only thing you

could think of to help." Rory spoke softly, her dark sorrowful eyes on my face as she finished my sentence.

I wanted to hug her or turn to Bash with accusing eyes and demand to know why my soulmate didn't understand what my best friend did without my having to explain. Instead, I nodded and spoke around the sick emotion trapped in my throat. "I just wanted to help."

"Well," Daniella moved further into the room and took a seat at her brother's desk. "Regardless of our motivations, although, I can admit that I was feeling completely sidelined, too, which is why I went along with it, we found out something pretty valuable."

Bash's eyebrows shot up. "What do you think you guys found?" His voice came out low and rumbly which prompted a look of surprise from Daniella.

She eyed him for a moment without speaking, then glanced over at me and back at him. I held my breath and hoped Bash would show some decorum and keep our grievances private, even from his twin sister. Although, from the gleam in her eyes, so like his, I knew she was well aware of the tension, now.

"Benson's involved in whatever his grandfather is up to and I can assure you that they're not planning Sunday tea parties." Daniella reached into her purse and drew out a tube of lip gloss. "That asshole loves nothing more than to brag about every single little achievement he's ever made. The fact that he clammed up and walked away without putting Elena and I in our subservient female place..." She slicked her lips with the gloss and made a smacking sound, leaving her sentence unfinished but the sentiment clear as a bell.

Bash made a dismissive sound. "You can't know for sure. Maybe he had something else on his mind and you could be reading into this completely wrong. Or," he glared at her and shook his head, "he is involved, and he's already alerted his grandfather about the two nosy girls on campus who tried to weasel details out of him." His voice rose in anger and visibly raised Daniella's hackles.

It felt good to see her react to his criticism in the same way I had. I understood that Bash was feeling left out and protective of both me and his sister, but he was being a fucking ass about it.

"You weren't there," Daniella snapped. "And I don't know if you've noticed, but we're not idiots." She gestured towards me. "We let Benson start the fight and just played into it enough to get what we needed. And if it can help The Sisterhood find out who murdered and kidnapped our sisters, then it was worth it. I don't know what bug crawled up your ass today, but you should probably dig it out." Daniella huffed and swiveled away from her brother, whose face had turned a dark shade of purple.

The room was silent for a long moment, then Connor, who I'd completely forgotten was in the room, cleared his throat and offered up his take on the subject. "I know you're being protective of them, man, but they actually did pretty good. There's no way Benson sees this as a fact-finding mission." I stared at him in shock for a moment then, seeing Daniella's smile of thanks, offered mine, too.

Bash looked at me through narrowed eyes then turned and leveled his gaze on Connor. The tension that had been present since before they joined us ratcheted up, until it was so thick it made the vein in Bash's forehead pulse. Beside me, Rory finally clued in that something was happening and turned to look at me with silent questions in her eyes.

I shook my head infinitesimally, never taking my gaze off Bash's face, which is why I knew what would happen a split second before Bash charged across the room with an ear splitting roar and slammed his fist into Connor's face.

CHAPTER 17

The crunch of cartilage breaking beneath bone filled my ears, followed immediately by a shout of shocked revulsion from Daniella, a loud gasp from Rory, and the thundering cacophony of my racing heart. Even the whispers paled in comparison.

They exploded like wild animals, punching, kicking, snarling, and throwing one another against walls, and chairs, and the door.

I'd seen fights before. Old Ones, I'd been in fights before, they weren't unusual, especially with young wolves. But I'd never seen anything like this before.

Connor fought back, throwing his weight into each punch and block, but there was a coldness in his eyes that was the complete opposite of what blazed from Bash's emerald depths.

There was madness there, and uncontrolled fury that twisted my gut painfully, because I knew what was at the root of it. I knew that every pent-up emotion Bash had held back from sharing with me was pouring out of him, right now, released at last.

This wasn't going to end well for either Connor or Bash. I swallowed hard and knew it wouldn't end well for me, either.

Somehow, one of them managed to open the bedroom door, spilling their brawl out into the hallway. Students parted like the Red Sea, shoving back against the walls to get away from flying fists and elbows.

I heard shouts of, "Stop that right now!" from multiple sources, but my head was spinning so fast, and the voices were chattering so incessantly, that I couldn't keep track of what was real and what was just inside my head.

Tears streamed down my face, falling helplessly to wet my shirt as I staggered after them, following the destruction wrought by the man I loved and the boy I used to love before I understood the true depths of love.

By the time they burst out of the dorm building, both Bash and Connor were bloody and limping, their lips swollen, their skin mottled with bruises that would heal quickly despite the pain that caused them.

Daniella and Rory flanked me, keeping me upright when my legs threatened to buckle. They spoke to me, reassuring me that everything would be fine, wolves sometimes fought, Bash loved me, and it would soon be over. I heard the words, registered them, but my body and mind felt numb, cold, and unable to accept that anything would be alright after all this.

Outside, what I thought was brutal turned vicious. Bash and Connor faced off, shoulders hunched, and fingers stretched wide as if they were the werewolves of Hollywood, grotesque monsters with claws and fangs. Bash snarled, pulling back his lips as he narrowed in on Connor, and threw back his head and howled at the night.

He threw himself forward and, faster than I'd ever seen, shifted into his wolf.

Connor's wolf leaped forward. I saw the change in his eyes as he embraced his nature and released his humanity. Fear surged through me at that look in the realization that this could very well turn into a fight to the death. And for what? Me? I lurched forward and felt my hands and knees on the ground, then vomited up the meal Bash had so thoughtfully gotten for me.

Daniella leaped back, saving her boots, and reached for my hair while Rory sank to the ground next to me and gently patted my back.

I raised my head and stared in horror as my soulmate leaped forward, tackling Connor to the ground, then chased him across the grass, towards the forest.

They disappeared around the corner of the next building, propelling me off my knees and into a dead run after them as the world swarmed around me hard it felt bruised against my ribs.

We didn't see them disappear into the tree line, but the sound of them, the gnashing of teeth, the howls, the sound of muscle hitting trees, filled the evening air with terrifying violence.

I wanted to run in after them, to physically grab them and pull them apart, stopping this insanity that would do nothing to ease the frustration and anger that my soulmate so obviously felt. Maybe Rory and Daniella were right. Maybe they did have to fight this out to find some peace and balance. I had to trust that they would keep their humanity enough to not go for the kill.

But how could I do that? Bash had cracked and, really, who could blame him? After the attack on campus in the fall and then the not so accidental plane crash that devastated our school and left him with questions about my honesty when it came to my past with Connor. How could I have been so stupid to think that he was coping with all this stress better than I was? Had I been so wrapped up in my own problems all this time that I hadn't even noticed he was drowning?

I shook my head and squeezed my hands into fists as I stared into the tree line, listening to the sounds of battle. I'd thought the connection between us had been a foolproof way to assess his balance, although saying it like that felt too clinical, too sterile. I was his mate and I would always want to know that he was alright. The realization that he must've hidden a great deal of what he felt from me, hit me like a blow to the stomach.

Did I even know my soulmate at all?

Panic welled up in my throat, blocking off my oxygen, and I gasped for air and answers I couldn't demand any more than I could stop the fight. I clutched at my throat and dragged in ragged breaths as everything I'd pushed down, layer upon layer of denial, rose to the surface and hit me like an avalanche.

The whispers that had faded into the background as I'd listened to the sound of howling and teeth biting into fur covered flash intensified, surrounding me with a cacophony that buffeted my senses. Only, this time, it wasn't just sound. Flashes of images filled my mind, playing behind my eyelids like a movie on a screen.

I saw them, the faces of the students that had stared up at me, eyes wide in disbelief that they would never again see their parents or loved ones, that they would never live another day, find their soulmates, or grow old and experience the joy of watching future generations grow under their watchful eye.

I felt their fear and confusion, and it wrapped me in a voice that squeezed until I thought my ribs would break and puncture my heart. Surely, I deserved that. I'd brought death to their peaceful existences. No, I hadn't tried to, hadn't wanted it, but the guilt that I tried so hard to shed, was still there, like an oil slick beneath my skin. It poisoned me, stealing the innocence I'd taken for granted once upon a time. I thought that I'd stopped that, taking things for granted, but I guess I hadn't.

Bash was hurting and I'd taken his mental health for granted. I'd been wrong about so many things, but being wrong about my mate's well-being, that was unacceptable. Even if he'd tried to hide his true feelings from me, I knew he would have done it to save me from an additional layer of guilt and stress. He was a good man and I thanked the Old Ones for the blessing of him in my life. I dragged in a deep breath, finally steadying my racing heart, and put my trust in my mate. Immediately, the storm of confused voices and images dulled and faded.

The fight went on forever or, at least it seemed to. It

drew a crowd, complete with frowning professors and grinning students. Someone mentioned campus security and ran off to find help, as I stood between Rory and Daniella, accepting their offered hands and support, and waited for Bash to do what he needed to do.

Eventually, the sounds quieted, and my heart caught yet again in fear that someone, either Bash or Connor, had gone too far. I knew Connor was the better fighter, he'd been training his entire life, but technical ability didn't necessarily trump passion and Bash had been furious beyond reason. I squeezed my friends' hands tightly and prayed.

"You'd know," Rory murmured next to me. "If anything happened to Bash, you would know."

I tore my gaze from the tree line and looked down at her, not fully comprehending what she meant. As it sunk in, I breathed out a sigh of relief. Bash might have blocked the connection between us at the level that let us share thoughts and emotions, but I still felt him out there, still knew he was alive. I let my eyelids flutter shut and pushed my awareness past the line of faceless whisperers to search for him and, when I found him, pushed everything I was into our bond in the hope that he'd feel my love, support, and regret, and come back to me.

My shoulders sagged and relief when I saw Bash, battered, and bruised, bloody but not completely broken, step out of the forest with a grin on his face. The tension in my shoulders released when, a moment later, Connor stepped out of the trees with an identical grin on his face. As I watched, Bash reached out and casually punched

Connor on the arm, laughing when Connor cursed and cradled the appendage.

"What the fuck..." I muttered, glaring at the two of them as they picked up the pace and jogged back to us, apparently all buddy buddy now.

"Men," both Rory and Daniella murmured at the same time. I agreed wholeheartedly with their assessment. Men were weird creatures.

When they reached us, Connor grinned at Bash and tilted his chin up, then looked at me without a hint of the coldness that had sapped away any sign of the boy I used to know. His husky blue eyes were lit up with a laughter and lightness that had faded a long time ago.

"Your mate has a mean right hook," Connor said with a chuckle, rubbing his arm again. His gaze moved past me, past Rory, and settled directly on Daniella. "Hey," he said with a sideways grin. "Does that mean you've got a good arm, too?"

Daniella eyed him with raised eyebrows, dragging her gaze over him from head to toe, then looking him straight in the eye as she shrugged. "Guess you'll just have to find out." She smiled, glanced down, then looked back up at him through her thick lashes.

She was flirting with him, I realized, with a start. I wanted to poke Rory, who was watching them with narrowed eyes and the barest hint of a smile on her lips, but there were more important things to do right now. We'd talk about the flirtation later. I turned away from my friends to face my soulmate.

"Are you alright?" I whispered, not sure what to say. I

opened and closed my hands, scrunching the fabric of my jeans, as my emotions churned.

He nodded, never taking his intense gaze off me, and took a single step forward, bringing his body close to mine.

I tensed all over, not afraid of him, but afraid there was still hurt inside him, caused by me. I squeezed my eyes shut and lowered my head.

His forehead touched mine, gently resting against the slope of my head and rocking up until our noses grazed, then shifted more until his lips brushed, ever so gently, over mine and inside my mind, the connection he purposely blocked, opened like a flower in spring.

I'm so sorry. I love you. I heard his words and felt the truth of them echo through me and back out, completing the circle between us.

I folded into him, bringing my arms up to wrap around his neck as we clung together, ignoring the crowd around us that were quickly dispersing now that the fight was over.

"I guess I've been burying some stuff," Bash murmured against my ear.

I shifted back just enough so I could look up into his eyes. There was still sadness there, mixed with hurt, and pain, and remnants of grief. I recognized the emotions intimately. They were the same ones I saw every day when I looked in the mirror.

"I guess we're not perfect." I freed my hands from the back of his neck to wipe a dribble of blood from his hair-line. "We have a lot to talk about." I rested my head on his shoulder and closed my eyes, coming to terms with the fact that I'd finally have to tell him and others the truth or risk losing my mind completely.

In his arm, my heart ached, but the voices seemed to quiet, just a little, as if they understood how devastating a decision that was.

CHAPTER 18

I sat in front of my laptop screen facing Sylvie and held my breath, convinced I was about to get yelled at. I forced myself not to look away, I'd done something wrong and now I needed to face the consequences.

Sylvie tapped her lips with the tip of her finger and said nothing for a long moment. "And you think Benson is involved, after all?" Her gaze stayed steady on mine, unblinking, giving away no hint of her reaction. It was incredibly unnerving.

I nodded. "Definitely. Benson takes every opportunity to boast about his family and he hates me more than most women, which is saying a lot because he's a misogynistic asshole." I cut myself off there because I was digressing, babbling because of nerves. "Daniella agrees. We think he knows something but, whether or not it's involved with the attack on The Sisterhood, there's no way to tell."

"Yet," Sylvie said, arching a single brow. "There's no way to tell, yet." She lowered her hands and smiled. "You can breathe now, Elena. I'm not going to kick you out of The Sisterhood because you spoke to Benson."

I blinked slowly. "But you told me not to do anything about it. Aren't you mad?"

Sylvie chuckled. "I might be your Alpha, Elena, but I'm also a mother of four. I don't think I could count the times my children specifically did something I asked them not to do. And, it isn't as if you broke my instruction. From what you've told me, you and Daniella orchestrated a casual run-in that just so happened to result in information useful to our investigation. I think you two handled it very well. Men like Benson, like his father and grandfather, assume they're smarter than everyone else around them, especially women. I doubt he even registered what happened."

Relief flowed through me, like cool water on a hot day. It calmed my heated cheeks and settled my stomach. "Still," I said, lowering my eyes for a moment in a show of respect, "I'm sorry. I wanted to help and didn't know how else I could contribute."

Sylvie sighed. "Oh child, I didn't even think about how hard this would be for you. You've been through so much this past year. It always surprises me how well you seem to be coping but, perhaps, you've grown too good at disguising your weaknesses. You know," she added, once again tapping her lips. "Being strong doesn't mean not having weaknesses. Have you ever heard of Kintsukuroi?"

I shook my head.

"It's a Japanese art form and method of mending broken pottery. You see, even the most sturdy or beautiful pieces of pottery eventually break, that's just the nature of their existence. But, instead of throwing away the broken shards when they do break, practitioners of Kintsukuroi, which I believe translates to golden repair, reassemble the pottery, using gold and lacquer to mend the pieces together. After, despite having been broken, the pottery is made even more beautiful not in spite of its weakness, but because of the way it acknowledges it was once broken."

She left it there, not spelling out the parable or proverb or metaphor or whatever the hell it was, and just trusting that I was intelligent enough to understand what she was saying. I did understand. It was our imperfections, once acknowledged and mended in some way, that made us more than we were before. I didn't have to be perfect to be strong, I just needed to stand up and admit that I needed help.

I licked my lips and took a deep steadying breath then confessed all my weaknesses.

♀ ♀ ♀

I stayed in my room most of the day, working on assignments, adding a few hundred words to my novel in progress, meditating from time to time or just ignoring the weight of the world on my shoulders.

Bash and Daniella were off campus for the day, visiting with their parents who had flown in for an impromptu visit. Bash had been frustrated when I'd refused to go with them, he'd hoped to finally tell them he'd found his mate and introduce us. The fact that they still hadn't met me in person and didn't know we were soulmates was yet another guilt that rested squarely on my shoulders. With everything that had been going on, I just hadn't wanted the stress of dealing with parents, mine or his. The only people who knew, really knew, that we were bonded, were our closest friends and mentors.

I knew he was close with his parents and wanted nothing more than to share his joyous news with them but the thought of it overwhelmed me every time and he respected my feelings. I wasn't sure how much longer he'd continued doing that on this particular front, especially since I knew it made him feel like a liar.

I'd kissed him and looked into his eyes this morning before calling Sylvie to confess and made a solemn promise to stand by his side tomorrow and tell his parents. I'd also wrangled a promise out of him to stand by my side while we told my parents immediately after.

When a knock came at my door, I wasn't surprised. After my confession to Sylvie, which had filled her eyes with worry and pinched the skin around her mouth, she'd admonished me for waiting so long, then consoled me while I teared up and tried to explain how afraid I was that I was losing my mind.

But she hadn't sent men in a white van to collect me and throw me in the loony bin. Instead, she told me to expect a visit from Dalia and to know that she and Katherine were thinking of me. She'd stayed on the video chat with me for over an hour even though I knew her time was incredibly valuable, especially in the midst of this terrorist attack against The Sisterhood.

Dalia stood in my doorway, dressed in old faded jeans, hiking boots, and a thin leather jacket with her hair pulled up in a messy bun. She looked effortlessly beautiful and fresh, despite being over five hundred years old. I only hoped I'd look half as good at that age and felt my youth intensely in the moment.

"Come on," she said, flashing me a smile filled with bright white teeth. "Let's go get some fresh air."

She waited while I pulled on a similar outfit, choosing sneakers over hiking boots because I hadn't brought my battle-scarred boots from home.

Like me, Dalia didn't quite fit in at Alpha Wolf Academy. She was far more in tune with nature than with snobbery and fancy education. That was probably why I liked her so much. Still, I knew that, like Sylvie, she wouldn't be pleased with my omissions. She'd warned me about the whispers, told me how afraid and alone she'd been when they'd started, then grown out of control. She'd offered me help and guidance and I'd still held back. Now, I had to face her and ask for her help. I grabbed my cell phone, tucked it into my back pocket, and took a deep breath to steady myself.

"Dalia," I said, turning to face her where she sat in my reading chair, casually flipping through my latest Sarah J. Mass book.

She looked up without saying a word and waited.

"I'm not sure how much Sylvie told you, but..." I searched for the right words to explain and came up empty. "I started hearing the voices, the whispers, after the plane crash. When you told me about them, you said, "at least you're not hearing the whispers," and all I could think was..." I lifted my hands and let them fall helplessly at my sides. I didn't know how to say this.

Dalia rose to her feet, putting the book on the bedside

table. "You thought you were losing your mind and that if you told me, I would tell Sylvie, and we would pull you out of school and put you in a padded cell. Does that summarize what you're trying so hard to tell me?"

I swallowed hard and nodded.

Dalia moved to the door and pulled it open, gesturing that I should follow. "Come on, then. We've got a lot to talk about and you've got a lot to learn."

We were silent as we moved across campus but as we stepped into the forest and surrounded ourselves with nature, Dalia began to speak.

"When I left my family, I'd been hearing the whispers for years. They started so slowly, and I just thought my conscience had gained a voice, one I didn't understand, but, that's it. I noticed, after a while, that they got louder whenever I was stressed out or overwhelmed, but my life wasn't particularly stressful at that time, so it was a gradual thing, like boiling to death."

I grimaced at the simile.

"Because I didn't know what was happening, it got so bad that the line between reality and madness blurred, then disappeared completely. I grew power drunk. I would lash out with my power at the tiniest provocation, whenever I felt anxious or frustrated. It was like a really horrible coping mechanism." Her eyes were dark with memories of those times.

I took a deep breath and asked the single question that was at the root of my terror. "Am I too far gone? You told me before that you had to go away to learn how to control it, that you were gone for years." I pressed a hand against my mouth and prayed that wouldn't be my story, too.

"I lost everything." Dalia stopped and braced her hand on a tree trunk. "My children lost their mother, I became a monster to them, to Jacob, to myself. But, Elena," she pushed off the tree and turned to look at me with fervent intensity. "You don't need to go through any of that. Yes, you should've told me right away. It would've been easier on you. I could've taught you how to focus and see them for what they are."

I frowned. "What are they really?"

A ghost of a smile flitted across Dalia's face. "Natural born Alpha's are different from those created by the Alpha Council. We are born with the power, even if it spends years hidden. Our power comes from the earth, from the elements around us, from the air, the water, the earth, fire, even the upcoming lunar eclipse. If you think of the way fiction depicts witches, say, and the way they are tied to the elements. That's probably the most accurate description of where our powers come from."

Dalia started walking again, further into the forest, reaching out to touch trees and plants as they passed. "The earth remembers. So, when a natural born Alpha begins to connect with their elemental powers, those elements flow through them and bring memories."

"What kind of memories?" I asked.

"Well, it might not seem like it now," Dalia said glancing over at me as she plucked a pinecone from the ground and began running her fingers over it. "But, those whispers, which, believe me, I know, are sometimes more like shouts, are actually memories."

I stopped walking and frowned, remembering the incoherent murmurings of the voices. I'd tried to block them out, and I'd tried to understand them, but they never got clearer. A thought occurred to me. "Did you only hear voices? Or were there images, too? Like flashes on a screen, really fast but detailed."

Dalia nodded. "I saw images, too, eventually, but in the beginning, there were only the voices."

My heart sank.

Dalia noticed my expression and crossed the small distance between us to take my arm. "No, Elena. Just because your experience is different than mine doesn't mean that you're going to suffer the same way I did. For starters, you're much younger and you haven't lost control, yet." She pulled back a little and eyed me. "Have you?"

I shook my head immediately, then remembered the first time I'd used my Alpha voice. I'd screamed at Benson and Grey to stop and had ended up driving everyone to the ground in agony. I was ashamed it happened, but I was done keeping secrets. "I didn't try it," I confessed. "And I didn't even know I had power to begin with. It was the first time and it never happened again."

"What happened?" Dalia asked.

"One of the guys in the plane crash got mad and was about to attack me, so I yelled at him to stop." It seemed such a ridiculously simple explanation, but that's exactly what had happened. "I screamed and lost all sense of reality for a minute. But when I snapped back, they were all on the ground, looking at me..." It had been horrible, the looks on their faces. The agony I'd caused. My stomach twisted with nausea.

"Is that it? Was that the only time you lost control?"

I frowned and thought about the last few months. Slowly, I shook my head. "That was it. I've gotten mad since then, but it hasn't happened again."

Dalia patted my arm. "Then I think you're going to be just fine." She began to walk again, so I followed.

"Here." She gestured towards a small clearing, thick with spring grass. Dalia sunk down onto the grass and crossed her legs, then waited for me to join her. "Let's try something. Take my hands."

I reached out and linked my fingers to hers, connecting our palms.

"I want you to close your eyes and feel nature around you." Her voice was calm and soothing, like the time we'd meditated together. "Feel the grass and earth beneath you and the soft wind moving through the air. Smell the new flowers and the scent of wet earth."

I focused on her words and let myself sink into the moment. I could smell the sap from the trees and the scent of wildflowers nearby. In the distance, water trickled over rocks, making a tinkling sound that lifted the corners of my lips. I felt the earth beneath me in the grass tickling my legs.

"Open your mind to the voices," Dalia murmured.

When I stiffened, she repeated the instruction.

"Open to them. You spent all this time trying to block them out or focus through them, now focus on them. But, relax, and think only of the elements around you."

I breathed deep and made my shoulders relax.

It was strange, facing the voices head-on, welcoming them but not really focusing on them. I did as Dalia had asked and breathed in nature, letting it fill me with peace and strength.

A voice, feminine and soft, lifted from the murmurs in my head, in a sweet song. My first instinct was to turn my thoughts to her, to focus completely on her, to figure out why the sound of her voice, singing a simple, childish song, made my heart lift and expand. But, I exhaled, and shifted my weight against the earth, feeling the coolness beneath me, connecting me with the elements.

An image formed in my head, the colors faded, of a woman with soft grey eyes and beautiful red hair. She looked down at me with a contented smile on her lips as she sang words I didn't understand.

Because they were Russian.

My eyes flew open and the image disappeared. The whispers swallowed up the single voice as I stared in shock at Dalia.

"Who was that?" But I already knew.

"Who do you think it was?" Dalia tilted her head to the side and studied me.

I swallowed and barely noticed the tears that sprang to my eyes and spilled down my cheeks as I whispered, "She was my mother."

CHAPTER 19

"It feels wrong, selfish to go forward with the party when those women are still missing," Daniella said as she pulled a gorgeous blood red cashmere sweater over her head and folded it neatly. "Don't you think, Elena?"

"What?" I blinked in surprise. "Sorry, I was thinking about something else. What were you saying?"

Daniella undid the button of her jeans and began shimmying out of them. "I asked what you thought of going forward with the birthday party, given everything that's going on right now." She glanced around at the students who milled around and I understood she didn't want to mention the super-secret sorority we were members of aloud in public.

I chewed my lip for a moment, thinking it over. We'd been planning a big birthday party but had gotten distracted lately and had put off the final details, like inviting anyone. Daniella had merely scoffed when I'd brought up that small point several days before I had just said that no one would turn down an invitation to her and Bash's birthday party, even if the invitation arrived one hour before the party was supposed to start. The exclusivity of it, she'd said with a saucy grin, would make the invitations even more sought after. Still, I'd gotten the feeling she'd been hesitant to go forward with the event and wasn't in the least surprised to hear her say something.

"Right. Well, we still haven't invited anyone, so there won't be any disappointments if we cancel. And even if we do cancel the big party, that doesn't mean we can't do something smaller, more intimate for just close friends."

The safety logistics of a smaller group would be easier to handle, I thought, glancing over at Connor, who was already down to his boxer briefs and just far enough away from us to not be obviously guarding anyone. I wondered for a moment how he managed to get away with being constantly close by but never actually attending classes. Didn't anyone ever notice?

Daniella noticed him; I knew that for sure. Maybe I'd only just started to pull my head out of my ass, but I'd been noticing a lot of little interactions between them lately. Daniella had never blushed so much in all the time I'd known her than she had in the past few days. Of course, Bash seemed completely oblivious to it and I wondered if he'd take any kindlier to Connor being in a romantic relationship with his twin sister then he had to Connor being my ex-boyfriend.

Everything had changed between the three of us since the epic battle that had been the talk of campus for days. The awkwardness and anger I'd held towards Connor had somehow completely dissipated. Bash and I had talked for hours about our feelings and insecurities, and had somehow, amazingly, strengthened the bond between us. I glanced around, looking for him, and caught sight of him waving goodbye to Darius, who still wouldn't look in Rory's direction, a fact I knew pained her greatly.

Bash caught my gaze as he jogged across the field. He let loose a long, low wolf whistle at the sight of me in just a bra and panties and took no time to begin pulling off his clothes.

"It's been way too long since our last run," he said, his voice muffled through the fabric he pulled over his head then tossed on top of Daniella's sweater.

Daniella glared, picked up his sweater and folded it neatly, muttering beneath her breath, "Men."

Bash ignored his sister completely and began taking off his pants.

"What were you guys talking about?" He asked, automatically pushing his sister back when she shoved him.

I grinned as I watched the interplay between the twins. They were so easy with one another, so real and normal. Yet, it had taken me a very long time to see anything but the shiny Queen bitch Daniella had projected when we first met. Not that it had been a projection, she'd actually been a huge bitch to me until I'd saved her life. Even then, she'd still been a bit of a bitch.

But fate had thrown us together more than once and we'd been forced to come to terms or die out in the Idaho wilderness after the plane had gone down. We'd chosen to live and things had only gotten better from there.

"We were trying to decide what to do for your birthday." I watched Bash strip off the last of his clothes until he stood only in underwear and took a moment to appreciate my soulmate's fine ass.

"I just don't think it's right to throw a party considering..." Daniella trailed off. "Plus, it would be hard to maintain security at a big party." She said it casually, but I clearly heard Connor's concerns in the comment.

Bash nodded. "Makes sense. Maybe we should just put it off this year, Dani. We've been having big parties every year forever."

"Or," I piped up, "We could do something small and intimate. Friends and family only."

Bash glanced across the field to where Darius chatted up another of their friends and I got the unspoken message. If I was there, Rory would be there. And if Rory was there, Darius wouldn't go. I bit down on my bottom lip and sighed.

"It's your birthday, Bash. Rory will understand." A buzzing sound coming from the pocket of my jeans pulled my attention away for a moment and I dug into my pants to get my phone. My parents had said they'd call sometime this weekend, but they knew the lunar eclipse run was tonight.

“It’s Xavier,” I murmured, checking the text.

Can you meet with me tomorrow to go over your manuscript?

I frowned. He’d told me he was busy this week and we’d made plans to meet up later next week to go over my progress. I’d written a new chapter in between bouts of deep thinking and mild depression and wanted his take on it.

Sure, I typed out quickly. *What time?* Immediately, I realized Daniella would need my help planning the new, smaller party all day tomorrow.

"Shit," I muttered.

"What's wrong?" Bash frowned.

"Nothing serious," I reassured him. We'd gotten way too much bad news lately. We were all a little jumpy at the first sign of trouble. "I just told Xavier I'd meet with him tomorrow about the book but I'm going to be busy with party plans all day. I'm just going to let him know I can't do it tomorrow."

"Don't be so foolish," Daniella chided. "Go play with your book. I'll take care of the party." She placed her hand on her hip and struck a pose, which looked insanely good since she was in just her underwear. "I'm a professional, you know."

"I can help, if you need it," Connor said, moving up to our little group. He usually hung back but, lately, he'd been joining in more often.

Daniella pinked up again and dropped the exaggerated pose. "Don't you have to watch Elena?"

Connor shrugged. "Yeah, but she'll be fine with Xavier for a few hours. I'll arrange another watch." His icy blue eyes stared intently into Daniella's emerald eyes.

Beside me, Bash stiffened. I bit back a giggle and tried to distract him. This wasn't the time or place to suddenly become aware of his sister's new flirtation and start another fight with Connor.

The first howl rang through the air just then, tugging at my heart. I tucked my phone away, grinned at Bash, and pulled off the rest of my clothes, anxious to feel the night air on my fur.

Tonight was a special run due to the lunar eclipse and what we called the blood moon. The pull of the moon on our primal instincts was always high but there was just something about an eclipse that filled me up. I looked up at the sky through slitted eyes and glimpsed the coming celestial event.

The eclipse was already underway but, now, as the sun, moon, and earth aligned, the reflection of the sun on the moon turned it a deep red that made emotion well in my throat. I leaned in and kissed Bash then called to my wolf.

She came immediately, moving through me like an ancient, primal, force that exhilarated. As always, the shift was accompanied by pain, but I'd never hated that part of the shift. For me, it was like the pain was a bridge that signaled my total transformation. It grounded me and connected me on a deeper level to my wolf.

I stretched my body out, arching my spine and ruffling my fur. Bash nuzzled me, running his wet nose along the line of my jaw. I glanced over to check on Daniella's and Connor's progress and saw them standing shoulder to shoulder, touching intimately.

A happy yip alerted me to Rory's approach. She loped over with Addison by her side, and head butted me then did a quick footed shimmy that made me laugh.

Seeing Addison as her wolf brought back a wave of guilt and pain that I immediately tried to push down so it wouldn't ruin our night. I stopped as the whispers in my mind began to intensify and squeezed my eyes shut. Acknowledging my weaknesses would make me stronger.

I opened my eyes to see Addison watching me, her expression deep and troubled. I realized that my pain had opened her wounds. Acting on instinct, I moved to her and brushed my cheek over hers in an embrace. She leaned into me and sighed in relief.

The sound of paws hitting the earth in unison, of hundreds of wolves racing into the forest, spurred my wolf forward. My muscles bunched and launched me forward, towards freedom and the simplicity of nature.

I lost track of time, of where we ran, of where we stopped to rest or drink or play. Everything that had been weighing me down, all the stress and fear and grief, floated away. Even the voices quieted as I ran with my mate and friends. I never wanted to stop.

We cut across an open field and slowed to look up as the blood moon faded, leaving only an eclipse that we couldn't look at. I remembered Dalia's teachings and reached out to embrace the elements around me.

The earth beneath my feet pulsed with life and the promise of spring. The air was fragrant and cool. I felt the strength of the world around me and the moon above me and opened myself to its power.

The sound of a baby's cries filled my mind, followed by the soothing murmur of a mother's voice. My breath caught in my chest as an image formed again, this time so familiar, and I watched as my mother smiled down into her arms and rocked me.

I felt her love, felt it pour from her into me, a reassurance that nothing would ever hurt me.

My heart squeezed painfully. Something had hurt me. Someone had hurt me. I'd been ripped from those arms by the actions of a mad man who still hunted me and haunted my nightmares. The bittersweet moment, a memory Dalia had said they were, faded away as if blown by a breeze.

I exhaled and stepped forward to rejoin my friends, who were further across the field than I, then froze as a scream ripped through my mind.

My body went cold all over, frigid with fear, as agony danced up my spine, bowing me back, and I heard the sound of breaking bone and gnashing teeth. I stared in horror and tried to shut out the image that played like a nightmare before my eyes.

Blood, so much blood that it sustained the earth and covered my hands. And Bash, lying at my feet, his eyes big and glossy, unseeing, and dead.

CHAPTER 20

I lifted the beer bottle to my lips and took a long pull, wishing the alcohol could wash away the memory of Bash's blood staining my hands. It wouldn't work. Nothing had managed to tear that image from my mind since it had ripped through my serenity the night before.

I still didn't know how I'd managed to finish the run without breaking down and blubbering to Bash and my friends about what the voices had shown me, but I'd put one foot in front of the other and made it back, then gone straight to Dalia. Only, she hadn't been there, and she hadn't answered her phone when I'd called. So, I'd laid awake all night, next to Bash, who'd slept soundly, and replayed the vision over and over until I had to climb out of bed and hide in the bathroom because I was shaking so hard.

It wasn't a memory, obviously. Bash had never laid at my feet, covered in blood and lifeless. So, what did it mean? Dalia had mentioned that the connection we natural born Alpha's had to the earth sometimes resulted in visions of what was to come. My stomach roiled once more at the thought that I'd been sent a vision of my soulmate's death.

But the future wasn't static. I believed that with everything I was. Yes, my world revolved around fate and the notion that there was one person out there meant for you, the other half of your soul that would complete you, but that didn't mean that you didn't have a choice. Actions always have repercussions; my mother had always said that. And choices created branches in our fate, that created multiple paths for the future. I wasn't a student of theoretical mumbo-jumbo, but I was sure that what I'd seen was only one possible outcome of the choices I'd make.

But which choices would lead to Bash's death? Which choices would leave me covered in his lifeblood, alone and broken?

Maybe it was just a manifestation of my fear, I reasoned again. I'd gone over all these possibilities endlessly during the night. I'd been so exhausted in the morning that I'd even cancelled my meeting with Xavier, then turned my phone off and put it in my night side table. Connor hadn't asked questions when I'd headed back to my room and told him I would be sleeping all day, but I'd seen the worry in his eyes. Eventually, my brain had shut down and afforded me a few hours of blessed oblivion. Then the nightmares had woken me and I'd spent hours meditating to find a semblance of balance even though I was now frightened of what the voices would show me.

Bash's laughter rang through the room, bouncing off the glass ceiling that let the light from the night sky in. I watched him, so light and happy with his friends, and couldn't imagine a world in which he didn't exist.

I finished off my beer and made my way across the room, which was filled to brimming with ferns, trees, and beautiful flowers. Daniella had outdone herself with this new location. I'd had no idea we even had a horticultural department at Alpha Wolf Academy let alone a luscious green house.

"This place is beautiful," I said, tossing my bottle into the recycling bin and grabbing another.

Daniella smiled. "It is, isn't it?" She looked around, stopping briefly on Connor, who was tucked away at a table in the corner, quietly enjoying the party. "Connor actually suggested that. I didn't even know it existed until this morning."

Deciding that a distraction was exactly what I needed, I arched a brow knowingly. "So," I said, drawing out the single word with a great deal of innuendo. "You and Connor..." I let it hang.

Color bloomed beautifully on Daniella's cheeks, matching the rose-colored sheath dress she'd chosen for her birthday party.

She bit down on her lip and exhaled long and slow, then turned to face me squarely. "Okay," she said, reaching out both hands and taking me by the shoulders. "I know it's a bit weird, but you're just going to have to suck it up. I really like him." Daniella's voice softened. "I don't know what it is about him." She shook her head with a laugh. "I can't stop thinking about him. I wake up thinking about him and dream about him every night. It's... I'm not used to feeling this way." She took another deep breath. "I'm sorry if this comes as a bit of a shock."

I tried to keep my face straight and serious. "I am shook," I said in a flat tone that only wavered a bit near the end. "Absolutely shook. I have never, in all my life, been so surprised as I am at this very moment." My lips twitched; I couldn't help it.

Daniella smacked my arm. "How did you know?"

I arched an eyebrow and grinned at her. "I'm sorry, do you think you're a master spy or something? You two have been making googly eyes at each other since the day you met. How did you think we wouldn't notice?"

Her eyes went wide. "Does Bash know?" She glanced over across the room at her brother, who was still grinning and laughing with his friends, then over at Connor who was watching her, his icy blue eyes warm now.

I nodded. "He suspects something but hasn't asked me about it just yet. But, don't worry, he and Connor seem to have come to some kind of an understanding. If he didn't kill Connor for kissing me after the plane crash, he won't kill him for kissing you now."

Daniella's smile disappeared. "Connor kissed you after the plane crash?"

I pulled back. "Shit," I muttered. "Yeah, he did, but, technically, he was concussed at the time and thought we were still together back home. Plus, his concussion was more or less my fault, so I didn't really give him hell for it. I didn't," I repeated. "But it turns out, Bash was a little pissed off."

"Okay," Daniella muttered, shooting me some side eye.

"As long as he was concussed." She dropped the evil look and grinned again, clearly happier than I'd ever seen her. "I'll forgive him for having faulty judgement while injured."

"Excuse me," Bash said, coming up behind me to slide his arms around my waist. "But I was just wondering if I could request the honor of your presence for this dance." He moved around me and held out his hand palm up, then bowed dramatically.

My heart warmed, chasing away the icy remnants of my vision. Bash was alive, whole, gorgeous, and mine. I placed my hand gracefully atop his and let him sweep me into the center of the room where a small area had been cleared as a dance floor.

We swayed together, his hands on my hips, my hands delved into his thick dark hair, completely in sync. I didn't know who had chosen the music, but I appreciated the current choice of Gavin Rossdale singing about love remaining the same.

I played with the hair at the back of his neck, giving it a little tug, which brought a gleam of awareness to his eyes that made me laugh.

"Down boy," I murmured, keeping my gaze locked on him. "You're just gonna have to wait until after the party for that kind of present."

The awareness intensified and his fingers tightened on my hips, before gently smoothing over the curves of my body. I gave him a moment to recover physically from my teasing and tried to ignore the scent of his pheromones in the air. There would be no controlling either one of us if we both gave into our hormones.

"I'm going to hold you to that," he whispered hoarsely, lowering his lips to mine.

The music picked up after that, so we joined Bash's friends in a game of beer pong, which, Daniella confessed, had been Connor's idea even though he couldn't play because he was on duty, technically.

I laughed more than I had in months and felt the ache of it in my sides, a lovely reminder of how happy I was with Bash. Even though the first blush of our romance, that uncertain time at the beginning of any relationship, was gone, it had been replaced by something more vibrant, more intense, and more permanent. He still made my heart skip a beat when he caught me watching him and there wasn't a day that went by that I didn't wake up wanting to see him. I blinked back emotion that was obviously alcohol-based and grabbed another beer, then a handful of my soulmate's ass.

It was a good ass. The best one I'd ever known. He didn't shy away. Instead, he reached back without looking, snagged me around the waist and dragged me around for a blistering kiss that made all of his guy friends howl in support. When we came up for air, I was breathless, pink cheeked, and more than a little horny. I shot him a look filled with promises and skipped away to rejoin Daniella and her friends.

Luckily for me, Daniella's friends no longer included the insufferable Serafina. Several members of what I had once dubbed The Bitch Squad, had dumped Serafina for Daniella, much to the new Queen Bitch's dismay. The others weren't half bad, especially once you got to know them outside the social confines of the popular girl group.

Like Daniella, they had real lives, real personalities, and real problems. I'd been learning that shiny objects only reflected what you thought you'd see, not what was really beneath the surface.

"Drink," Daniella commanded, handing me a shot glass filled with what could only be tequila.

Because it was her birthday and because I was wasted already, I threw back the shot and reached for a wedge of lemon.

"Wooo!" I cheered, wrapping my arm around her shoulders. "Hey," I said, turning Daniella so we were face-to-face. Her face was so pretty, I thought. Just like Bash's. "You're pretty." I booped her on the nose.

She grinned. "You're pretty, too." Daniella leaned in to whisper so loudly she might as well have just said it in a normal volume. "I'm really glad you and Bash are mates. Did I ever tell you that?"

I shook my head so hard it made the room spin, so I stopped and waited a moment. "No, you didn't, but that's so nice!" I looked over at Layla, who I remember thinking was perfection itself on my first day at Alpha Wolf Academy, and asked, "Isn't that nice?"

Layla nodded emphatically with wide eyes. "Yeah. Is Bash really your soulmate, Elena?"

I nodded proudly. "Yes, he is." I wrapped my arm around Daniella's shoulder again and squeezed. "Which makes me and her," I gave her a loud smacking kiss on the cheek, "sisters-in-law." I frowned. "That doesn't sound right. Soulmates in law?"

"Soul twins?" Daniella offered with a shrug.

"Well, whatever it is, we're that," I said with a decisive

nod then freed my arm from Daniella's shoulder and declared, "I have to pee."

Without waiting to see if anyone would join me, which girlfriends usually did, I headed out of the garden party to find a bathroom.

I found one halfway down the corridor and slipped through the door with a happy laugh, thinking about how great it would feel to relieve my bladder. I always thought about that when I was drunk, how great it felt to pee, and I always reminded myself to tell somebody. I decided to talk to Daniella about it when I got back to the party.

I was just fixing my hair by running my fingers through it several times, when the door pushed open and I turned to smile at whoever it was.

The light to the bathroom flicked off and I yelped, more out of instinct than out of fear. My eyes would adjust quickly to the dark. They didn't get the chance to, though.

All I saw before my world went dark was the outline of a man dressed all in black.

CHAPTER 21

The whispers woke me, dragging me from a dark emptiness into a world of pain and confusion.

I opened my eyes or, at least, I tried to. I felt as if they were welded shut but, after a few moments of straining against my body's desire to just stop fighting, they lifted just the slightest bit.

I groaned and pain exploded like a bomb inside my brain, cutting off my voice instantly. I squeezed my eyes shut and the effort caused only more pain. So, I lay there, wherever there was, and tried to breathe through the pain and fog, so I could think straight and understand.

It was cold here and damp. I knew I was in the dark. Again?

My mind struggled to hold onto the pieces of memory. I'd been at Bash and Daniella's birthday party. I'd gone to use the bathroom. Then the door had opened and…

My breath hissed out as it came flooding back, that

brief second of awareness that I was in danger before everything had gone dark.

My breath grew shallow as panic began to set in. I knew what this meant. I knew exactly who was responsible for my abduction. And I knew what he would do to me.

Viktor.

My thoughts grew fuzzy again and I had the clarity to understand that I needed oxygen to think, to try to find a way out while I was still alone. I dragged in deep, ragged breaths and forced my body to relax.

I'd been here before, I told myself. Not here, exactly, but I'd been in a life-and-death situation, more than once, actually. Viktor had tried twice now to kill me, unsuccessfully. That stupid saying filled my mind in a childish singsong voice, *third time's the charm.*

I hoped not, because I didn't want to die. I didn't want to leave Bash.

Bash! He could find me. Our bond linked us. If I could just...

I reached out to him, opening myself to the connection of our souls and found nothing. *No,* I thought, as panic flooded my body, immobilizing me, not nothing. He wasn't dead. The vision I'd had of him laying bloody at my feet hadn't happened. He was alive, just nowhere near enough to reach.

Moving slowly, I tested my limbs and found them weak and bound by something strong. Rope, I thought, flexing my wrists against the fibrous material.

I was lying on something semisoft, a cushion of some

sort. I wondered why Viktor would give me such a small comfort when he was planning on killing me anyway.

Maybe it's not Viktor.

The thought rushed through my mind like a leaf on a breeze, there one second, then gone because I knew it was false hope. There was nothing more dangerous than false hope. The voices in my head must have agreed because they got louder at the thought.

I frowned. I hated the voices with a passion but maybe they could be useful. Just because I had never been able to control them in any way, didn't mean it wasn't possible. What if I could use them to see where I was or to amplify my connection to Bash? It was worth trying. What other choice did I have but to try?

The damp in the room reminded me of my grandparents' basement before they'd laid down a subfloor and carpet. It smelled musty, like old dirt, which was good. I was cut off from the outside down here, but I could still connect with the earth.

I rolled from side to side and heaved myself off the cushion, then smothered a curse when rocks bit into my exposed arms and legs. The scent of blood mixed with earth filled my nose.

A sacrifice, I thought with a grimace. My blood for some help.

I pushed my arms into the dirt and stone and tried to quiet my mind. It was hard, almost impossible with the specter of death hovering, but I pictured Bash in my mind, then Rory, Daniella, Sara, Bethany, my mom, my dad, and my grandparents. I moved through my loved ones, picturing their faces, until my pulse slowed, and I was steady enough to focus on the elements present in this dank place.

Earth, water, and air were here. I opened myself to them, welcoming the flow of their intrinsic power into me. Instantly, the clambering quieted until the voices were a gentle hum in the back of my mind. I tried to remember a time when my mind had been silent and couldn't.

Maintaining my even breathing, I relaxed my shoulders, my stomach, even my tongue, as Dalia had shown me, and sunk deeper into my awareness.

Fragments floated to the surface, snippets of my mother singing, flashes of her face, this time accompanied by the rugged handsome features of a man with startlingly beautiful electric blue eyes.

My heart ached, with grief and happiness to finally meet my father. I'd seen pictures of him, of course. It hadn't taken me long to Google the Dom Volkovs and see images of what my family had been. I'd been loved, dearly, and would have had a wonderful life if Viktor hadn't been hungry enough for power to stoop to murdering his own blood.

My stomach twisted and I forced myself to breathe through the pain. It would do me no good now.

Images of the past could be useful, I thought, as I tried to navigate past my parents so I could see Viktor and maybe find something that could help me fight back against him. But, no matter how hard I focused on his face, that horrible visage that visited me in nightmares, I saw nothing that could be useful.

I swallowed fear that tasted like acid. The past

wouldn't give me the answers I needed, which meant I had to look to the future. The image of Bash, covered in blood, tugged at my consciousness, but I pushed it away. I needed help, *Old Ones, please*!

The whispers intensified at my frustration, swirling chaotically as I pressed into them, searching for one face, one voice, and nearly sobbed in relief when he finally swam to the surface.

She cannot be allowed to live. He spoke to someone I couldn't see. His eyes blazed with purpose, a mission, a single goal. Wipe out all competition to the Alphaship of Russia and solidify his future.

She's just a girl, his companion said in a voice that sounded oddly familiar. *I don't understand why you're so afraid of her.*

I felt rage explode through Viktor, a flash of heat so terrible it nearly singed me. He struck out, with fist and voice, all fury and indignation that anyone would dare to question him.

"I am afraid of no one!" he roared and his face distorted, changing him from handsome to demonic.

I gasped and the image of him faded, just a little, enough that my fear of him was forced to morph into fear of losing this chance. I struggled to refocus and breathe.

Viktor grabbed the man, I could tell it was a man now, by the shirt and jerked him to his toes. *You ask a lot of questions for someone who has so much at stake. Perhaps you'll choose to save this little girl instead of your own.*

I felt the man sag in Viktor's hands and knew that whoever it was would no longer stand up for me. I was on my own. Completely and utterly on my own.

No, I stiffened. I couldn't think that way. I couldn't just give up and stop fighting. People had died protecting me, ensuring that I alone out of my entire family would survive. I couldn't just give up.

I pressed harder, drawing the elements around me into my body, searching for more inside the confusion.

Viktor's face sharpened and his emotions, dark and dangerous, snapped into vivid clarity. I latched onto the image and searched for something, anything, that could potentially save my life.

The sound of heavy footsteps on the floor above me, making the wooden boards creek as they passed, had all my effort going up in smoke. Terror overtook me and I twisted to look in the direction of where the footsteps stopped. The sound of a door being unlocked brought vomit to my throat, where it burned and stole my breath.

The door opened, letting in a brilliant wash of light that illuminated the single figure standing at the top of a long set of stairs. He stood in relief, a figure of darkness, cast in the shadows of the light.

Viktor.

I began to tremble as he descended the stairs, slowly coming closer, his outline wide at the shoulders and narrow at the hip. I struggled to breathe, to think, to do anything other than barely hold back screams. I wouldn't scream, no matter what he did to me, I wouldn't give him that satisfaction. He'd already taken too much from me. My innocence, my security, my family. He wouldn't take my pride; I wouldn't give him that.

I pulled back my lips and snarled.

"Coward." I snapped my teeth at him, wishing I had my

canines so I could sink them into his throat and rip it out. The bloodthirsty thought didn't shock me. I was a wolf, after all.

"Elena, I'm so sorry."

I frowned. I'd heard Viktor's voice in my dreams night after night, so I knew his voice intimately, though I wished I didn't.

That wasn't his voice but it was one I recognized.

"Xavier?" I asked, barely able to contain the hope that sprang into my chest.

He was silent for a moment, dulling the hope, then he squatted down before me and answered. "I'm so sorry, Elena. Please, believe me. I'm so sorry."

The hope died a violent death.

I shook my head, it didn't make any sense. "What do you mean, you're sorry? What's going on? Why are you here? Please," I begged. "Help me. Untie me. Viktor..." I trailed off.

Xavier didn't move, didn't reach for the rope to release me, didn't so much as breathe. He knelt there, hovering over me as my eyes adjusted to the new light and I finally saw his face.

His eyes were downcast, unable to look at me, and his face, so handsome, had aged since I'd seen him last. He looked haggard, frail, and afraid.

"You?" I asked as my mind raced to catch up. It didn't make sense, none of it made sense. Xavier was my mentor, my professor. He couldn't be helping Viktor. He wouldn't. I opened my mouth to ask a million questions but only one thing came out. "I saved your life."

He sobbed out a ragged breath. "I know, Elena! Old

Ones, I know, and I'm so sorry, but he has them." Xavier reached out and grabbed me by the arms, shaking me until my teeth rattled. "Viktor has Annabelle and Jayelle."

I choked back a gasp. His daughter and ex-wife. His office was full of pictures of his daughter, so bright and beautiful and, obviously, the apple of his eye. His face lit up whenever he spoke of her. Now it seemed to crumble beneath the weight of her abduction.

Understanding soothed my confusion and the whispers, which were more like angry screams now. He would sacrifice everything for his daughter.

He would sacrifice me.

I looked away from him and let tears stream from my eyes, knowing what little hope had sparked at the sight of him, was now gone forever.

Xavier pushed to his feet and, once again, murmured his apologies, but they were just to assuage his guilt. They meant nothing to me. He was doing what he had to do to save the most precious person in his life. I didn't blame him, not really. I blamed Viktor. He was the sick mastermind pulling all the strings.

A dark heaviness filled my limbs, dragging me down to the earth so that it felt like I'd never be able to move again. My mind grew heavy, too, then began to float, leaving the fear and pain behind. Faced with fight, flight, or freeze, I was freezing to death.

I didn't move when a buzzing sound broke through the silence. I didn't blink when I heard Xavier answer the call with, "Just a minute."

And I didn't breathe when I heard Xavier open the door and usher Viktor into the room.

CHAPTER 22

A sharp garish light flicked on overhead, blinding me.

I winced and squeezed my eyes shut, then listened as Viktor walked down the stairs, slowly and with more menace than I'd thought possible in footsteps, then strode across the large room and stopped in front of me.

"I did everything you asked," Xavier said in a shaky voice, edged with desperation. "Where are they?"

Viktor chuckled. "So anxious."

The sound of his voice, that Russian accent, echoed inside my mind like a nightmare. It made my blood run cold.

"They will be returned to you when my work here is complete," he said so simply I almost didn't understand at first.

His work. The blood drained from my face, bringing nausea and a faint ringing that joined with the whispers to make me lightheaded. I was his work. Finishing the job he started more than twenty years ago, when I'd been just an infant. How callous and insane did one have to be to refer to murder in such a casual way? I wondered if it would be quick, at least.

I half expected Xavier to apologize again for his betrayal, but he left the room without saying a word, then clicked the door shut, leaving me with my uncle.

For a long moment, Viktor didn't speak. I laid on the floor, bruised and defeated, with my eyes shut against the sight of the face I now recognized from memories gifted to me by the voices. I'd known already from pictures that there was a strong family resemblance between the two brothers, but seeing Viktor now, after glimpsing my father's face, filled with love and life... it was heart wrenching. A tear squeeze from beneath my eyelashes and dripped onto the ground.

"Poor little wolf," Viktor practically purred. "Don't cry." His voice changed in an instant, sharpening like claws. "It's not becoming of a Dom Volkov."

His chuckle sent ice down my spine. "Your mother cried. She woke as I drove the knife into your father and knew the truth, just for an instant, before I took her life, too."

Their faces popped into my mind, unbidden. I shut them down, quickly, as quickly as I could, because they were beautiful and young, and I didn't want to watch them morph into what he was describing. I would join them in death soon and, hopefully, reunite. Until then, I wanted their smiling faces to remain the only memory I had of them.

My silence annoyed Viktor, I could feel it radiating from him in the way he moved, stalking back and forth with his eyes burning into my flesh. I prayed my refusal to play into his games would prompt a quicker death.

I wasn't that lucky.

Fingers drove into my hair and twisted viciously, then yanked me up. I screamed; I couldn't help it. The sound tore from my throat. No matter how hard I tried to hold it back, it came.

Viktor backhanded me, sending me sprawling across the room. My face hit the dirt and rocks hard, knocking my teeth together, sending pain flaring through my head. I gasped for breath and tried again to free my hands and feet from their binds. It was no use, though. Xavier must've been a Boy Scout. His knots were unbreakable. Betrayal twisted my stomach. I turned, lifting my face from the ground, and vomited what little was left in my stomach.

"Tsk, tsk, little wolf. I know you weren't raised properly, but I would think something of the noble blood line that runs through your veins would have come through. Surely, you're stronger than this. Where's the girl who fought her way across campus and never gave up, even when faced with death?" His voice rose in question that sounded sincere.

I gritted my teeth together, determined not to respond to his taunts. What was the point? If I pissed him off, maybe he'd prolong my death, just for fun. Or, I thought bitterly, maybe he'd do that anyway, because, after all this time trying to kill me, he wouldn't want it to be over too quickly.

Fuck it, I thought. If I was going to be tortured anyway, I might as well have my say first.

"You don't deserve to speak of my parents." I spat blood and stomach acid onto the ground, rolling to glare up at him. "You stole into their rooms in the dead of the night and murdered your own family. Don't speak to me of nobility. Nobility is more than brute strength."

His foot connected with my abdomen a second later and I heard a ripping sound from deep inside me. Blood sprayed from my lips as I gasped for breath and tried to decide if my wolf's healing abilities made me lucky or cursed. I'd heal from the impact; it wouldn't speed up my death. No, it would just hurt like a son of a bitch while he inflicted more torture.

Still, it had felt good to lash out at him with words, with the truth. I doubted anyone ever told him the truth. I looked up at him, at the gleam of madness in his familiar blue eyes and smiled.

"What's wrong, Uncle?" I managed to say through ragged gasps. "Are you so afraid of a little girl like me that you'd keep me tied up and battered instead of facing me like the Alpha you claim to be?"

My words twisted his face into something primal and ugly. Fear skittered down my spine, but I couldn't stop myself anymore. If I couldn't fight back with fists and teeth, if I couldn't avenge my family that way, the least I could do was rip him a new one with my words.

"I bet they all bow down to you," I hissed, trying not to cringe back as he stepped forward, drawing back his leg to kick again.

He froze, holding back the fresh torture and bared his teeth. I took the opportunity.

"Maybe you're okay with that. Maybe that's the kind of

Alpha you want to be. But you and I both know that's not what an Alpha is." I spat more blood in his direction. "You don't deserve the title or the power."

Viktor roared and drove his foot into my stomach again. I heard bone break and felt searing agony. My world went blindingly white for a split second then the light was swallowed up and my mind shut down.

♀♀♀

I woke to the sting of a slap that snapped my head back sharply. I blinked in confusion and squinted up at the outline of a man hovering above me.

"What…?" I mumbled, turning my head to look around the unfamiliar room as my head swam with confusion and the insistent sound of anxious whispers. My lips were dry and cracked, so I licked them, and the coppery taste of my own blood on my tongue brought reality flooding back. My stomach cramped with emotion, fear, anger, guilt, and, strangely, relief.

I frowned. Why relief? It made no sense. I didn't want to die, didn't want to face the man who had murdered my family and threatened my life and the lives of my friends for months now.

"Welcome back, little wolf." Viktor stepped away from the glaring light aimed directly at my face so that I could see him clearly. His lips lifted in a mockery of a smile as he looked down at me. "I thought we'd have some fun before…" He chuckled. "Well, before I kill you, to be frank." Viktor leaned over me. "You wouldn't want me to pretend, would you?"

I took a deep breath, drawing in the scent of him and wishing I was free to hunt him down like the prey I wanted him to be. Slowly, I shook my head. "No," I said through gritted teeth. It would be worse if he pretended I had a chance.

I tested my binds and found them still there and, possibly, even tighter than before. My skin was rubbed raw at each site, coating the ropes in blood that dried then was refreshed as I struggled and bled anew.

Sickened by the sight and scent of him, I turned my head away and caught sight of a window where there'd been none before. I scanned what I can see of the room and realized I wasn't in the basement anymore.

I was above ground and lying on something hard and wide. A table, maybe. I narrowed my eyes to avoid the blinding light still aimed directly at me and twisted my head to look at the other side of the room.

The gleaming metallic surfaces and cold air were that of an industrial kitchen, something like a restaurant would have. I eyed the block of knives sitting on a nearby counter and knew they'd be sharp. At least they wouldn't be silver.

The thought of silver drew my gaze back to Viktor, who'd moved away and had his back to me. He and his mercenaries had used silver bullets during the attack on campus in the fall, so I knew he wasn't averse to using the poison against his own kind. Hell, he'd proven he had no qualms about killing, period.

Katherine had been tortured once, I remembered. She'd mentioned it but hadn't gone into gruesome detail other than to say that she understood the pain I'd experienced when one of Viktor's silver bullets had torn through my thigh. I hadn't asked. Even though we were friends now, I figured torture reminiscing could be saved for a later date. We'd never have the chance to commiserate now.

"You know," Viktor said, turning back to me was something in his hands that I couldn't see. "As much as I want to rip your throat out and watch you bleed out right here, right now, there's something I want more." He opened his fingers and held up a clear glass vial of powder. "Do you know what this is?"

My gaze centered on the vial and the grey dust filling it. Sweat beaded on my skin as I understood that I'd been wrong once more. "Silver dust," I whispered in horror. Panic chased away all reason and I fought against the ropes, twisting, and screaming, until the scent of blood filled the air and my voice broke.

Viktor watched me, his blue eyes gleaming in delight. He wanted me screaming and begging, he wanted to watch me bleed and die, and I had no power to deny him what he wanted.

When my voice went hoarse, he put the vial down and pulled on a pair of gloves, to protect his own skin from the silver, I realized. There would be pain now, endless, mindless pain.

"What do you want?" The questions scraped from my raw throat. "Why are you doing this?" I knew that he wanted me dead because of my birthright and the threat I posed, however small. But I had no idea what else he wanted out of this. Whatever it was, I just want to know.

He snapped one of the gloves at his wrist and grinned.

"Why am I doing this," he mused aloud. "Well, little wolf, you see, your death isn't the end of this for me. You should've died with your family all those years ago, but you were secreted away by a maid, or so I'm told. And do you know who it was that told me this little fact?" He lifted his eyebrows and looked at me, waiting for an answer I didn't have.

I shook my head, just trying to keep him preoccupied so the pain wouldn't come as soon.

He stared down at me, then reached out a gloved hand and smoothed the hair away from my forehead. "You're so beautiful. I suppose you know that, though. Beautiful women always know." He coiled my hair around his finger and gave it a gentle tug. "You have your mother's hair and delicate features and your father's eyes, *my* eyes," he added with a smile. "It's unnerving, seeing them looking back at me." His smile disappeared. "That's why they'll be the first to go."

His forearm descended and trapped my head in place. My eyes went wide in terror as he flipped the top off the vial with his other hand and moved closer to my face. Sick understanding flooded me as his words sunk in and I screamed again, squeezing my eyes shut.

It didn't help. His hands, so strong, held me down as I bucked and struggled to break free. He didn't stop to lift my eyelids, there was no point.

Silver dust fell onto the thin skin protecting my eyes, instantly engulfing me in indescribable pain. I screamed and begged the Old Ones for death.

CHAPTER 23

I didn't lose consciousness.

If I could have prayed, I would have. I would've begged the Old Ones to let me fall into the blissful abandon of unconsciousness. Instead, the silver dust burned through my eyelids and attacked my sight, destroying it in a single, careless moment.

Silent screams shredded my throat as I writhed in agony, struggling against the ropes to free my hand so I could… I had no idea what I could do to stop the pain, but I had to do something. It pushed me, beyond sanity, to the very brink of breaking. I didn't know how I managed to stay on that ledge and not leap, maybe there was a serenity there, beyond the breaking point. Something kept me there, though, poised on the precipice as the whispers turned to screams that buffeted my mind and soul.

They seemed to want something from me, but it was impossible to know what. It was impossible to know anything but red-hot searing pain.

Something speared into my hair, pulling me forward to the end of the table. I wrenched oxygen into my lungs, able only to sustain the barest minimum of consciousness. Then, the oxygen was gone, and my head was submerged beneath icy cold water that sucked into my mouth and down my throat, drowning me.

The burning in my eyes dulled beneath the water surface, releasing me for a moment from that exquisite agony while my broken ribs screamed. I would drown instead, I thought, and admitted to myself that it would be better. But, as soon as the thought entered my head, I was being pulled free of the icy water and thrown back onto the table. Something hard struck me in the middle of the back, and I coughed up the water I'd swallowed, then laid there gasping for breath.

The light that had blinded me earlier still pointed in my direction, I could feel its heat, but I couldn't see its light. Tears, bitter and futile, streamed down my cheeks. I didn't know how I could cry when my eyes were so destroyed.

I felt Viktor move closer to me and cringed away.

"There," he murmured, stroking my face through his gloves. "That's better. Now we can talk." He disappeared for a moment and I heard the scraping of a metal chair against the floor. He sat heavily and leaned in again. When he spoke, he sounded as if he were having a polite conversation with an acquaintance. "Tell me about The Sisterhood."

My heart stuttered. I hadn't considered that his "talk" would involve those I loved. True, he hadn't asked me about my family or my friends, or even Bash, but The

Sisterhood, however much I'd resented them when I'd discovered their role in the deception of my life, they were my sisters. Katherine, Sylvie, Daphne, Rose, and all the other amazing women I'd met were important and vital. I didn't know why he cared about them, about hurting them. I assumed he wanted to hurt them, anyway. He destroyed everything he touched.

I opened my mouth and tried to speak, but only a croak came out.

Viktor made an aggravated sound. "Can't answer questions if you can't speak," he muttered. "Never mind," he patted my arm encouragingly. "We'll just have to go with yes and no questions for the moment until that pesky throat heals up."

I shuddered out a gasping breath.

"Did you know, little wolf, that you had an aunt?" Viktor asked. "Well, technically, you still have an aunt, she's just rather indisposed at the moment." He tapped his fingers against the table. "You see, I thought I could trust her, but it turns out she's been a member of this silly sisterhood of yours all along. It also turns out she knew of your existence." He made a tsk tsk sound. "It was unpleasant, punishing her, but very necessary. Even though she denied knowing anything, she actually knew quite a bit and all it took was a bit of coaxing to get it out of her." He leaned close enough so that I felt his breath hot on my face. "I wonder how long it'll take me to pry every drop of information from you. It took my sweet Irena two days to divulge all she knew."

My stomach heaved again but there was nothing in it to expel so I just spasmed while he watched.

"Alright, then," he began, and I knew it was time. "Let's start with something simple, shall we? Are you a member of The Sisterhood?"

Some small stubborn and spiteful part of me wanted to shake my head no, but I refused to listen to it. He obviously knew I was a sister. If I lied, I'd be punished, tortured again and again. The longer I could hold off from that pain that threatened my sanity…

I wasn't sure how to finish that thought. Maybe it was better to push him fast and hard. Maybe I'd save myself unnecessary agony. Or, maybe he'd keep me alive for days and amuse himself either way. He'd just admitted to torturing his own wife for two days, after all.

I nodded and tried to say the word yes, but all that escaped my throat was a wheeze.

He patted my arm. "Good girl. Now, something a little harder. Do you personally know Sylvie LaFlamme and her daughter, Katherine?"

Tears poured from my ruined eyes as I nodded again.

"Good. Now, tell me, do they trust you?"

I froze in place. He'd admitted to hating The Sisterhood, to wanting revenge, and wanted to know if two high-ranking members trusted me. Through the pain, my mind cycled through everything he'd said and came to one conclusion.

He wanted to use me to get to them.

Steel stiffened my spine. There was no way in hell that I would betray The Sisterhood. Sylvie and Katherine were like family to me now. I'd endure endless torture and still refuse to help Viktor harm one hair on their heads. I clenched my jaw and refused to answer.

"So, we've come to an impasse. Our first. Let's celebrate, shall we."

I knew what would come and braced for it, but when the silver dust sprinkled like deadly snowflakes on my already exposed eyes, my body arched into the air, and I heard the snap of bone.

I existed only in my head. The voices wailed as the silver burned my eyes, destroying the proof of our familial resemblance. I couldn't think, couldn't breathe, couldn't remain on that precipice any longer. Without a second thought, I leaped and let the whispers drag me under.

It was better beneath the surface. The pain still existed, but I was separate from it somehow, like an astral projection floating just outside the body, looking down at it as it died.

Viktor let me burn then dragged me to the water and pushed my head beneath the surface again and again, washing the silver from my eyes. With each dunk, the whispers calmed and wavered, then voices, single voices began to ring through, clearer and urgent.

Confused desperation flooded me as Viktor dragged me back up onto the table. There'd been something there, in the water, in the darkness that brought salvation. I tried to think, tried to remember, but it just kept slipping away.

My hair splayed across my face, soaking wet, reminding me of something, a shadow in a dream. Then a voice, so familiar it hurt, called my name and I strained to listen.

"You'll have no eyeballs left, soon," Viktor said with a

snarl. "Then what will I move onto? We'll need your throat in working order soon enough, so I suppose..." He trailed his finger down my body but I barely noticed. In the darkness it was quiet and I could think.

He bombarded me with questions, one after the other, barely taking a breath in between. I stayed silent and still beneath the force of his fists and palms, beneath the sting of his nails and knives. And when silver sprinkled over my forehead, I focused on only one thing, touching the water.

I was prepared this time when he pushed my head into the icy liquid. The voice that had pushed forward, refusing to be ignored, spoke to me as clearly as if she were right next to me.

Open yourself and see.

I opened to the water, connecting with the element with every ounce of strength left in me, and it responded. Time seemed to slow. Viktor's hand, pushing me further into the water, moved in slow motion, giving me time.

An image formed in my mind, foggy at first, then clearer with each passing moment. Hope leaped in my soul, eclipsing the pain of my body, as I watched myself stand before my oppressor, battered, bloody, yet no longer blind. In the image, Viktor was staggering under the weight of my power. In the image, I was free from these ropes and fighting back.

And I was winning.

CHAPTER 24

Time lost all meaning.

I drifted in and out of consciousness, each time lifted by Viktor so that he could ask more questions and punish when I refused to answer.

My body burned all over, his silver dust did its job and did it well. From the darkness where I floated, free from the brunt of the agony he caused gleefully, I wondered how long my physical being could remain alive after such torment.

It was strange, this disassociation, but I was aware enough to be thankful for it. In my psychology classes, we'd discussed trauma dissociation. When fight or flight wasn't an option, freeze took over. That's where I was now, frozen in my mind, in a sort of holding pattern where the hope birthed by my vision could survive the endless pain of Viktor's torture.

I noticed small things, like the way Viktor muttered to himself when he was frustrated and the way he favored his left hand. I couldn't see him as he used his fists to batter me, but I could feel the strength of his right hand as it held me down.

The sun set, stealing the small warmth that had filtered through the window. At one point, seething at my stubbornness, Viktor had knocked the spotlight over, so that I lay now, shivering and alone, in the darkness.

Guards came and went, checking on me, to see if my rope still held or if I was still breathing. I counted them, six different scents, six different foot falls, six different presences that ignored my plight and did as they were bid.

I fell asleep eventually and dreamed of my friends and family, frantically searching for me in the forest under the light of the blood moon. I tried to scream, to call out that I was still alive, still fighting, but my voice was locked away in a box that I held in my hands. Voices squeezed through the cracks of the box, whispering for me to never stop, never give in.

I awoke to the glare of the sun on my face and nearly abandoned my place in the darkness when I realized that I was seeing light, not just feeling it. My eyes were healing, slowly but surely, and would recover if given the chance. Viktor would never give me that chance if he found out, but it meant that my vision was coming true. I'd be stronger soon.

I didn't flinch when the door opened, and I heard the familiar fall of Viktor's footsteps coming into the room.

"It's a beautiful day, little wolf," he said in a voice that was surprisingly chipper. "New day brings new opportunities. You surprised me, you know. I expected you to crack a long time ago but maybe there is more of me in you than I thought." He stopped next to the table, blocking out the light from the window.

I stared up at the ceiling, as I'd done for hours the day before, and refused to let him know that my sight was returning, however minutely.

Viktor ground his teeth together when I didn't respond. "I should've grabbed one of your little friends, too," he muttered. "That would get you talking."

Relief was like a warm breeze through my mind. If he was complaining about his regrets, that meant my friends and family were safe. I was surprised, though, that he hadn't taken one of them. Then again, I realized, he would've been confident enough in his skill to break anyone, to never see my silence as an option.

He sat in the chair next to the table and took a sip of something. *Not coffee,* I thought, I'd smell that. Water, maybe. At the thought, my mouth went incredibly dry and my tongue licked out to touch my cracked lips.

"Thirsty, are you?" Viktor asked, not moving from his seat. I heard the splash of water and the sound of his swallows. The only water I'd been given the day before had been from the bucket that had washed away the silver dust from my face. I'd held my breath most times, as the water had been filled with silver particles that, if swallowed, would attack my body from the inside. I either sated my thirst and helped my body survive, or swallowed silver and weakened myself further. It was a horrible choice, but I'd made it and now my body was healing, inch by precious inch.

"I suppose it wouldn't do to have you die of dehydration," Viktor said, pushing to his feet. He poised the water over my mouth and slowly let it drip onto my lips.

I took what he offered, not grateful, but relieved. Yes, my body was healing, but it would be a lot easier to heal if I weren't dehydrated. Wolf metabolism meant faster healing, but it also meant an increased need for fuel and they hadn't given me anything to eat or drink since I was taken.

He pulled the water away before I could quench my thirst, then, before I could swallow the last gulp, he covered my mouth and nose and chuckled as I choked.

"I think it's time we start again, don't you? I trust you're well rested and ready for a new day." I heard him shrug out of his jacket and hang it across the back of the chair. Preparing for the new day's work of breaking me down.

I wondered if there was a point of physical pain that would draw me out of the darkness and the safety of disassociation. I wished I'd studied the topic more, but there hadn't been a reason to go more in depth at the time. Who in their right mind would foresee a future where they would be tortured and then murdered?

I heard the slap of fabric on one of the kitchen countertops and tried to imagine what new agony Viktor had in mind for me.

"That silver powder we played with yesterday was fun, wasn't it?" Viktor called out. "I brought some more fun things with me today," he added, approaching. "A whole bag of fun things, in fact. Like this." The razor-sharp edge of a silver knife sliced into my forearm and dragged from my elbow to my wrist in one slow-motion.

My nerves lit with fresh torment and I retreated further into the darkness, letting the voices surround me, protecting me with their whispers.

Viktor asked the same questions he had the day before and, when receiving the same silent answers, began to lose his temper and slice rapidly at any exposed area of my skin.

My blood flowed onto the table, surrounding me with the scent of death. From deep inside the shadows, I began to question if what I'd seen had actually been a vision of what would be, or if it was just a figment of my imagination and desperation for hope.

The sound of metal clapping together, broke through my questions.

"I think it's time we start losing parts of you," Viktor growled. "I'm getting sick and tired of the silent treatment, little wolf. Maybe this will get you talking."

He grabbed my shoulder and yanked hard enough to turn me over, exposing my hands. I realized as he pulled my fingers apart and slipped something cold and metallic over the end of my pinkie, what he was about to do. My body tried to squeeze my eyes shut even though I still had no eyelids.

The door to the room flew open, hard enough to hit the wall with a bang, and one of Viktor's minions, a tall guy from the length of his strides, hurried across the room.

"What do you want?" Viktor demanded, pausing to yell. "Can't you see I'm busy here?"

"Sorry to interrupt, Alpha," the man murmured in a

low voice. "But they've caught our scent. If we don't move soon, they'll be on us."

The metal fell away from my finger and clanged to the floor. If I'd been any less detached from my body, I would've sobbed in relief. Instead, I forced myself to listen and understand what the guard was saying. The Sisterhood was looking for me and was closing in. If I could just hold on a little longer, there was a chance I wouldn't die.

Viktor roared and slammed his fist down on the table, just inches from my body, splintering its surface. The guard stayed silent while he raged, upending chairs and other furniture in the room, while I prayed and dared to hope. Maybe, just maybe, my vision wouldn't come true because it wouldn't be necessary.

When all that was left was Viktor's ragged breathing, the guard spoke. "What are your orders, sir?"

Viktor blew out a ragged breath. "We leave now."

"What about her?" the guard asked.

Yes, I thought. *What about me*?

Viktor laughed and the edge of insanity in his voice was more terrifying than any torture he'd already inflicted on me. "Go get everything ready. I'll take care of her."

My heart sank. The Sisterhood wouldn't find me in time. I have to trust that my vision would come true, not today, but one day. Holding onto that, I stayed calm as I was yanked around and up to my feet.

I thought he'd throw me over his shoulder and cart me off, possibly to a helicopter or private plane. I worried, for a moment, that I'd be thrown inside something dark and small, and calmed myself by remembering that I was already somewhere dark and small, inside my mind.

When I felt the tug of something on my ropes and I heard what sounded like a serrated blade cut across them, confusion filled me. Viktor was cutting my feet and hands free. The moment he let go of my hands, I crumpled to the floor, unable to stand on my own.

"Get up," Viktor growled. He reached down and grabbed my arm, wrapping his long fingers around my bruised and bleeding flesh, and pulling me roughly to my feet. "You might be the child of my brother, but there's too much of me in you to let you die on the floor like a nobody."

Shock punched through the darkness and wrapped its frigid hands around my throat. All around me the whispers turned to moans then screams that would have deafened anyone else, but I was used to them now. Or, as used to them as I could get without going completely mad.

I didn't want to die. I was too young, too new in this life that was filled with possibilities and experiences I hadn't had the chance to share with those I loved. I couldn't leave Bash behind. My death would crush him and, by extension, Daniella. I thought of all we'd been through, the distance we'd come together, and knew it wasn't my time.

I leaned against the table, hands braced behind me as the blood flow returned to my legs and lifted my gaze toward Viktor. The morning sunlight poured into the room, illuminating him from behind so that I could see his outline. The image I'd seen in the water pushed forcefully to the front of my mind in vivid detail and I saw

Viktor, through the vision, almost exactly as I saw him now.

This was it, then. This was what the voices had wanted to show me. The moment I made the connection, their screams faded, and excited murmurs took their place, like the whispers of an anxious crowd waiting for the big fight to begin.

I tilted my head to the side and looked at him, really looked at him even though my eyes were still barely functioning, as if I could see something more, beneath the surface, that I could appeal to. There was nothing there, beneath those eyes, beneath the skin that made him appear human, but actually disguised something sinister and cold. His eyes registered the change in my demeanor immediately and lit up with interest.

"Welcome back, Elena," he said with a grin that was all teeth. "You really are more like me than your father, you know."

My lips curled back. "I'm nothing like you. I would never betray my own blood like you did." I huffed in derision. "I've said it before, and I'll say it again. You don't deserve to rule."

His teeth ground together and a low growl emanated from deep in his chest. I flexed my muscles, urging the blood to resume its flow and give me back the strength I needed to fight. I needed time, but that was a commodity I didn't have. With The Sisterhood closing in, Viktor was eager to do what needed to be done, then leave.

I moved along the edge of the table, keeping my hands steady on the edge so Viktor would think I needed it to stay upright. I didn't, not anymore, but I didn't want him to know that yet. So, I moved around the table, putting distance between us, hoping that he would take that as an indication of my fear, and grow cockier than he already was. He hadn't taken any of my friends from campus because he'd been cocky. I'd use that against him, now, plus anything else I could think of.

"Where are you going, little wolf?" Viktor asked, stepping closer. His steps grew quieter but in the stark room it was impossible to hide the sound of his movement, especially now that my sight was impaired. It was true what they said, lose one sense and the others perked right up.

"Do you think I'd actually make it easy for you to murder me?" I spat the words out, letting the fury that raged in my veins flow through my question.

Viktor chuckled. "On the contrary, I was growing disappointed at how easy you were making it. This is much better." He stalked closer, coming around the other side of the table so we were separated only by a wide piece of wood and steel.

I tried to glare at him but that didn't work when you didn't have eyelids. So, instead I snarled and snapped my teeth. "What makes you think you can take me now?" I asked, loading my voice with as much derision as possible, just to piss him off even more. "You couldn't take me when you attacked campus. I've only gotten stronger since then." I wanted to brag about all my training, including my hours spent with Dalia, but I held it, deep inside, where he couldn't see. He'd never see it coming.

The table flew forward, crashing into my hip bones, sending me sprawling back several feet. I scrambled to stand up and locate him again through the haze of my blurred eyesight. He moved like the wild animal he was, crouching low and placing one foot after the other slowly, constantly aware of his footing and his prey.

I wasn't doing as well, I thought bitterly. In the vision I'd been standing in an open area and right now I was trapped between the end of the kitchen, the table, and the cabinets on the far wall. I needed to get around the table, but he had the upper hand. My sight was dull, my body was weakened from torture, lack of food and water, and lack of blood flow. He was smart, Old Ones knew he was devious, so I had to be better, smarter, stronger and the only way I knew how.

I had to use my Alpha power.

I'd never tried to use it against someone. When I'd blasted Benson and the group after the plane crash, I hadn't been trying to hurt them, I'd just been trying to stop them from hurting me. It had burst out of me, completely outside of my control, and taken down everyone around me, before I even understood what was happening.

I understood now what it was I wanted to do, but I had no clue how to access that kind of power within me. My time with Dalia had been spent trying to understand my natural born Alpha abilities, not learning to control it, not yet. I'd always planned to learn, but I'd thought that there'd be more time.

I inched back, away from the table, knowing that it would open me up to attack when Viktor rounded the corner. I needed him to think that I was vulnerable, without any way of fighting back, and panicking. It would lower his defenses and give me an opening, however small.

The whispers grew louder as I backed away, murmuring incessantly, warning me of danger. I reached out to them and the hum of energy that sparked to life as I opened myself, calling to anything within me that could help.

"Foolish little girl, thinking you can fight me." Viktor's voice was closer now and filled with the certainty of his victory. "What do you possibly think you have that could stand up to my power?"

It was the perfect opening. I couldn't have asked for better. Channeling Buffy, I cocked my head to the side, let my lips curve in a deadly smile, and screamed.

CHAPTER 25

Viktor flew through the air and landed hard against the edge of the table. His face twisted in shock, then rage, as he realized what was happening.

My throat had healed, my desperation and anger had strengthened me, and my Alpha voice had come when bidden.

It blasted out of me, never ending, building continuously so that my skin vibrated with its power. I dug my nails into my palms and bunched the muscles in my shoulders and arms as I strained forward, aiming the destructive power of my voice in full Alpha mode at Viktor's head.

He had his own power, and I knew it would only be a moment before the shock of my defense settled and he came at me with his. He'd had years to practice controlling the power that came with his position, so that gave him an obvious edge. But, from the look on his face now, I guessed that he'd had no idea what I was or what I was capable of.

I grabbed the nearest object to me that wasn't nailed down and threw it with all my strength, then darted towards the other side of the room and the open space I'd seen in my vision.

Viktor's roar was primal and tore from his chest so bitterly that it sent shivers of fear down my spine. I shook them off, refusing to succumb to his demand that I bow to him. That's what it was, that vicious roar. I recognized it and turned to face him and make my own demands.

Strength and sharp focus flowed through me, filling all the cracks Viktor had created with his silver and vicious words. The whispers in my mind cheered me on quietly, as if they feared distraction. My eyes, still shadowed and blurry, fixed on Viktor's outline as he shook off my attack and stalked forward with power and anger coming off him like waves of heat. I tried to blink, to wet my injured eyes, and nearly sobbed when I felt eyelids, newly formed and delicate, slide down to protect what Viktor had tried to take from me.

"I see you, you know," I said, offering him a twisted smile. "Which means that I'm healing, faster than normal even for our kind. What do you suppose that means?" I scanned the room through still blurry eyes, looking for weapons or impediments. I didn't want to trip over anything and lose this fight because of an accident.

He moved closer, keeping his body low and ready. I'd caught him off guard with my display of a power I shouldn't have access to, but he was highly intelligent and loved nothing more than collecting information that he could potentially use against others in his bid to gain and maintain his position. I doubted he was ignorant of the existence of natural born Alphas, even if I'd been before meeting Dalia. He was keenly intelligent, I knew, and would acclimatize quickly.

"So," he said conversationally. "You're a natural born Alpha." Viktor made a humming sound in his throat that was both fascinated and annoyed. "Very interesting. That explains how you withstood my attack at the academy."

That had been my first experience with an Alpha and the powers that came with the position. Viktor had used his voice to dominate and it had driven Bash to his knees. I'd suffered under the pressure of his mind, too, but I'd been able to move through it, slowly but steadily, like walking through waist deep wet snow. Katherine had been able to function through it, as well. I wondered if that had something to do with her being the child of an Alpha. Two Alphas now, I supposed.

"It's cute that you think that makes you my equal, though." I heard the smirk in his voice. "Let's see how you manage against real Alpha strength."

I barely had a split second to realize his intent before Viktor launched himself forward, fists high and lips curled back in a snarl.

Months of muscle memory kicked into gear and had me ducking beneath Viktor's fists and spinning out of his grasp. I came out of the spin with my leg pulled up and, using the momentum, snapped my foot out to hit him square in the chest.

Viktor staggered back and cursed savagely but caught himself before he fell to the floor.

I grinned and cocked an eyebrow at him just as I imagined the vampire slayer would, knowing it would piss him off even more. Buffy knew her shit and could get a rise out of any Big Bad. Anger would throw him off or, at least, I hoped so.

"I've been practicing," I said, impressed with my acting skills when my voice came out calm and confident. "But it looks like maybe you've let yourself go recently. Have you gained weight?" If I'd had eyelashes to flutter, I would have charmed like a Southern Belle. Instead, I smiled and danced back from a jab. He was around the same height as Tomas, so I was well versed in avoiding strikes.

"I've been fighting and destroying my enemies for longer than you've been alive, bitch," Viktor said smugly. "Some I ripped apart with my hands, some with my bare teeth. Others, like your parents, died at the end of my knife. Some are more worthy than others to die as warriors."

I bit down on my cheek and tried to hold back the grief and anger his words unleashed. I'd known he'd use them against me, like a weapon, so I'd braced for it, but it hurt all the same. He'd stolen lives in the dead of night like a thief and regretted nothing. He'd murdered children, his blood kin. He was a demon and needed to pay for his crimes.

My wolf surged forward, pushing against my consciousness, offering her strength without taking over. I couldn't shift, not now, it would leave me too vulnerable. His wolf was bigger than me, too, so it really didn't matter. Either way, we were unevenly matched.

"Yeah," I said through gritted teeth. I didn't care if he saw that his taunts made me furious. I just wouldn't let them distract me from my goal. "You've said that before.

You're repeating yourself, old man." When he growled, low and throaty, I shrugged. "You should have probably come up with some new material before facing me."

He moved forward like a snake, throwing his weight and strength into the attack. He was fast, but I was faster. I was also still seeing the world through a filmy layer, so my other senses would have to step up. I blessed Tomas' tyrannical ass for making me practice with a blindfold or in the dark on the regular.

I blocked a kick that would've sent me to the floor with broken bones but, instead, deflected off my forearm, leaving the bone bruised but intact. Viktor rained blow after blow down on me, tireless in his advance. I stood my ground, feet planted wide to absorb the shock of his punches and kicks and avoided as much as I could. Those that I couldn't avoid, I blocked.

Pace yourself. Let your opponent show off and grow tired, then attack. I heard Tomas's voice as if he were standing over my shoulder and slid to my right to avoid Viktor's battering fist.

He fought well, as any Alpha should, but he favored his left hand, even though he tried hard to disguise the preference. I didn't think I would've noticed, not in the midst of a life or death battle, but I'd noticed too much, or just enough, while he'd tortured me. I didn't know how I could use it to my advantage, but I kept it in mind. Viktor wouldn't blink at using someone's weakness against them, so neither would I.

My body ached, everywhere, and, to my dismay, was growing weaker with every passing moment. I was holding back, keeping my reserves steady, but I hadn't eaten in at least twenty-four hours, had only gotten small sips of water during that time, and had been battered, bloodied, and tortured. If help didn't arrive soon or if I didn't find a way to take Viktor out of the game, I'd lose everything.

He threw a punch that grazed my chin and spun me. I staggered back, keeping my fists high to protect my face, but he was too fast, too strong, and I didn't see it coming. Using his momentum, Viktor swung around, pivoting with his arm held high, and smashed his elbow into the side of my head.

Bright lights exploded behind my eyes, shattering my world. I felt like a stone to the floor as the room went hazy and Viktor's triumphant laughter burned my ears.

Get up! I shook my head, trying to brush off the confusion, and wondered who was yelling at me this time. It wasn't Tomas's voice and it wasn't the long-lost memory of my mother, either. It wasn't even one voice, I realized as I planted my hands on the floor and pushed to my feet.

It was a chorus of voices, all speaking together, all talking as one, and all saying the same thing.

Right jab, now!

I didn't think, didn't pause, I just acted. My right hand squeezed into a tight fist and dropped down to my waist, pulling back as my body pivoted and lowered, giving me the momentum I needed to fulfil the voices' instruction. With a scream of effort that ripped through me, I drove my fist into his ribs, which were unguarded and vulnerable.

The crunch of bone beneath my fist was like music to my ears. I wanted to cheer, to dance on the spot, but this was it, my opportunity. I threw out a mental "thank you!" to my inner coaches and grabbed for Viktor's head, sinking my fingers into his thick hair. With a vicious yank, I pulled him down until his skull made contact with my knee.

"Now we're fucking even!" I spat the words at him, barely noticing the blood that sprayed from my mouth. I was on my feet, that was all that mattered. The fight wasn't over yet.

The sound of helicopter blades approaching twisted my stomach in fear and hope. That was either The Sisterhood or Viktor's escape plans. Either way, this was it. Viktor wouldn't leave me alive, not again. Not if he could help it.

The door pushed open and one of Viktor's guards strode into the room, face set and eyes hard. "Our ride is here." He jutted a chin towards me and swung a familiar gun around, leveling it at my heart. "You want me to take the shot?"

Viktor hissed and waved a hand towards the man. "No! She's mine. Get out!" he roared the order and the man obeyed.

"You should have taken him up on the offer," I said snidely, wiping my mouth with the back of my hand. My head still rang painfully but I'd been through worse. The voices chattered again, incomprehensible but managing somehow to bolster my confidence. They'd helped me more than once and I trusted they would again. Viktor might know my secret but he didn't know about them.

Viktor laughed and spit on the floor. "I'm done playing with you, little wolf. You have spirit, I'll give you that, but you cannot be allowed to live." He pulled himself up to his full height, abandoning his fighting stance and drew back his shoulders. "You might think you have power, but you are just a child, playing with things you don't understand." He took a step forward, facing me without any distractions, and summoned his Alpha power.

The air filled with what felt like static electricity. It grew thick and heavy, scented with the tang of ozone as Viktor pulled from the gifts given to him when he'd stolen the position of Alpha from my father. He gathered his power, held it for a moment that seemed to waiver in time, balanced by the weight of the moment, then he released it.

His Alpha voice hit me with the weight of a stampede, trampling my head and shoulders as he reigned down orders that would have decimated an ordinary wolf under his command. I felt the impact of it and staggered but, where it would have driven another wolf to their knees, it only awakened what was inside me.

I reached for something to brace myself on as a shock of raw power burst from somewhere so deep inside my being I hadn't realized it existed. I wanted to quake, to shudder and cry out for help but, in an instant, it was filling me, driving out all thought of uncertainty.

"I am the rightful Alpha of Russia!" Viktor's face twisted in horrible convulsions as he shouted his claim, trying to use it to push me back, to deny me my birthright. He meant to use it as a weapon, but it only infuriated me. That he would dare to lie to my face!

"You are nothing!" I screamed back, balling my fists at my sides as my body shook with power that could barely be contained. It felt like I would be torn apart if I didn't let it out. I gasped for breath, wishing I weren't alone, but knowing there was no one else, besides Sylvie, who could be in this room and not be driven mad. The whispers in my mind were deafening now, raging screams that tore at my mind, tempting me back towards the darkness.

I wasn't prepared when Viktor lunged forward. I didn't see it coming. He wrapped his hands around my neck, digging his long fingers into my flesh as he leaned forward, aiming the full devastating extent of his power straight into me and squeezed.

His power hit me like a tidal wave, drowning out everything else around me so that only he and I existed, locked inside a struggle that would destroy one or both of us.

I grasped his wrists, but not to break his hold on my neck. From inside the wave of power he aimed like a weapon, intent on destroying what I was, the cacophony of sound and pressure disappeared, surrounding me in a silence so complete, I lost myself in it for a moment.

In the silence there was life and love, so perfect it rocked me to my core. I let it caress my mind like a loving mother and realized that, perhaps, that was exactly what it was. A gift of a moment with my lost loved ones, a place of peace where I would welcome death and what came after.

No, the voices spoke as one again, piercing the silence. *This is not your time. Fight, Elena. Fight, now, and win.*

I sighed beneath their words. It was so peaceful here in the silence. Outside, in the real world, I was broken and bloody, my mind was at war with itself, my body about to implode. If I just stayed here, if I just closed my eyes and stopped fighting, it would all be over.

It will never be over if you give up. Fight, now, and win, they repeated.

It would never be over, I agreed. Even in death, it wouldn't be over. Viktor had cheated, stolen, and killed for his position, and he was involved, somehow, in the attacks against The Sisterhood. My sisters were dying, paying for the protection they'd given me as a child and for all the world they'd accomplished over lifetimes so that girls, like me, could step forward and fight back.

No, it wouldn't be over even if I bowed out. The fight would never stop as long as there were people like Viktor in this world, free to use his power against others like a battering ram. I took one last breath, gathered myself, and turned back to the battle.

My body pulsed, already filled to bursting with the power that flowed from my bones, from my cells, from my soul, and from my connection to the elements. His power, the sheer force of it, hit me but, rather than pushing me down, it flowed into me, merging with the pulsing life within. Together, they melded, gathered, crested to a peak, and poised for a second as they pushed forward, too strong for me to hold back.

Not that I wanted to hold back.

I let go. It was as simple as that. Inside my mind, I opened a door, releasing a flood gate, then stood strong as the totality of it, too much to comprehend even as it surged through me, burst free.

A sound like a thousand thunder strikes filled the room, ripping from my throat, driving Viktor to his knees in an instant. His fingers fell from my neck and I threw my head back, purging the pain and fear, everything that had eaten away at me for months. It washed through me, emptying every dark hidden corner of my being, and then it was gone.

My head fell to my chest, too heavy for my neck to hold up. Bone deep exhaustion dragged at me, whispering that I was done, that I could sleep now. I watched through still-filmy eyes as Viktor's gaze locked on my face and his electric blue eyes went wide with understanding then dark as he fell to my feet, dead.

I loomed over his body, held up by invisible strings that stretched then snapped, one at a time, until there was nothing but stubborn pride holding me up. My body swayed, as if suddenly surrounded by a soft summer breeze that welcomed me home. It wrapped around me, bringing an explosion of twinkling stars and loving voices that encircled me, calling to me like long-lost friends.

I was safe now, we all were. Viktor was gone. I could rest.

I smiled into the silent darkness, letting it gather me close, then whispered Bash's name and left the world behind.

NEXT IN ALPHA WOLF ACADEMY...

Will the darkness keep Elena captive, or will she fight her way back? Find out in Bad Moon, the 4th book in the Alpha Wolf Academy series!

GET IT NOW!

A broken mind, a long road to recovery, a new threat from within, and a whole shitload of trouble.

Elena Jensen should be relieved, she should be happy, she should be free, but the powers she tapped into to destroy her greatest enemy came with a heavy price.

After months of training and therapy, she's returning to Alpha Wolf Academy, even though she isn't sure it's the best idea. Her future might be safe, but it's uncertain at best. The Sisterhood have been covering for her, keeping the Russian pack at bay, but Elena needs to decide, and soon, or risk anarchy.

Elena struggles to rebuild herself, to find control and her place, and is starting to feel like her old self when she's side railed by two new students who seems to be out to get her. Bash and her friends just don't see it, but Elena can't shake the feeling that she isn't safe.

Doubting your own sanity makes seeing the wolf at the door a little bit harder.

BEFORE THERE WAS ALPHA WOLF ACADEMY...

If you want to start at the beginning and meet Katherine LaFlamme, why not grab a copy of Blood of Eden, book one of The Guardians trilogy.

Trouble's brewing in the pack... and Katherine is willing to risk her life if that's what it takes to save her family.

When Katherine LaFlamme is summoned home by her father, the Alpha of the North American wolf pack, she drops everything and answers the call. Despite her desire to experience the human world before she settles down, Katherine is fiercely loyal and, as the pack's best tracker, she's an essential part of stopping the darkness encroaching on their territory.

A hunter has invaded their territory and murdered several of their kind, while a rogue wolf has been stalking the female members of the LaFlamme family. To make matters worse, a secondary claim to the Alphaship of North America has risen, setting the entire pack on edge.

Then Katherine meets a mysterious wolf named Quinn and things begin to get interesting... and very deadly. Katherine and Quinn are swept up in a puzzle of ancient rites, prophecies, and mythic lore which reveals that there's more to both of them than first meets the eye.

ABOUT THE AUTHOR

JJ King is the USA Today Bestselling paranormal loving alter-ego of author Janice Godin. She was born and raised on the beautiful island of Newfoundland and makes her home there still with her amazing son. She attributes her love for the supernatural to Buffy and is thankful there are so many other people, like her, who love a little otherness with their romance.
Oh, and she loves sushi and cats!

To find out more about JJ King and all her upcoming projects, check out her website at http://janice.godin.com

www.ingramcontent.com/pod-product-compliance
Lightning Source LLC
Chambersburg PA
CBHW020550020726
47494CB00006B/2002

* 9 7 8 1 9 8 9 7 9 4 0 4 3 *